'I did try to ***evening.'***

'A little late, wouldn't you say, when I've obviously already purchased the Old Vicarage?' he drawled.

'Just a little,' she conceded ruefully. 'But don't worry. If you intend staying, you'll soon get used to it.'

'Oh, I intend staying,' he told her flatly. 'But I also intend living here in quiet seclusion, and have *no* intention of doing anything that will give the villagers cause to gossip about me,' he added grimly.

Perhaps now wasn't the time to tell him that he wouldn't actually need to do anything to be the subject of gossip; just his being here at all, a well-known television star, already had the inhabitants of Aberton agog with speculation as to why he had bought a house here. The last Jaz had heard—from the postman this morning as he'd handed her her letters—Beau Garrett had come to the village to escape an unhappy love affair, when the woman in his life had left him following the car accident that had left his face scarred…

Carole Mortimer was born in England, the youngest of three children. She began writing in 1978, and has now written over ninety books for Harlequin Mills and Boon®. Carole has four sons, Matthew, Joshua, Timothy and Peter, and a bearded collie called Merlyn. She says, 'I'm happily married to Peter senior; we're best friends as well as lovers, which is probably the best recipe for a successful relationship. We live on the Isle of Man.'

THE VENGEANCE AFFAIR

BY
CAROLE MORTIMER

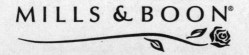

MILLS & BOON®

MILLS & BOON and MILLS & BOON with the Rose Device are registered trademarks of the publisher.

First published in Great Britain 2004
Paperback edition 2005
Harlequin Mills & Boon Limited,
Eton House, 18-24 Paradise Road, Richmond, Surrey TW9 1SR

© Carole Mortimer 2004

ISBN 0 263 84123 5

Set in Times Roman 10½ on 12 pt.
01-0205-45760

Printed and bound in Spain
by Litografia Rosés, S.A., Barcelona

CHAPTER ONE

'OH!' SHE came to an abrupt halt halfway across the moonlit terrace as a shadow moved out of the darkness only feet away from her, the pounding of her heart only lessening slightly as she recognized the man who stood there looking at her with the glittering eyes of a cat. She drew in a deep breath. 'Shouldn't the guest of honour be inside the house enjoying the party, rather than outside on the terrace—?'

'Enjoying the peace and quiet?' Beau Garrett finished harshly.

She had come outside herself in order to do just that. In fact, she had hoped that, once outside, she may just be able to slip quietly away without her hostess, Madelaine Wilder, being any the wiser. Bumping into the elusive guest of honour had not been part of her plan!

'They're looking for you inside,' she told him pointedly.

'Are they?' he returned uninterestedly, his overlong hair a dark sheen in the moonlight, his features shadowed. 'I'm hardly dressed for the role of guest of honour, am I?' he rasped impatiently, the casual sweater he wore looking black in the darkness, as did his trousers. '"Do pop in, I'm having a few friends over for drinks".' He mimicked a pretty fair imitation of Madelaine's gushing voice. 'There must be half the village in there.' He nodded disgustedly in the direction

5

of the audibly noisy house as people talked and laughed too loudly, their glasses chinking.

'At least,' she acknowledged, moving out of the shadows of the house to join him at the balustrade looking out over the garden, a garden sheathed in the mystery of March moonlight. 'I hate to tell you this, but this is the third drinks party Madelaine has given to welcome you to the village of Aberton—you just didn't appear at the first two!'

It was somehow easier to talk to this man in the covering of darkness, his sensuous good looks, the sheer masculinity of him that was so apparent on the small screen as he hosted the chat show that had been such a success for the last ten years, muted in the covering of darkness.

The grimness of his dark scowl wasn't. 'If I could have got out of this, without being completely impolite, then I wouldn't have appeared at this one, either!' he rasped.

If the way he occasionally ripped to verbal shreds his often controversial guests was anything to go by, then she didn't think politeness was necessarily a part of this man's character. In fact, it was the sheer uncertainty of what was going to happen each week on his live television chat show that made it so popular.

'Poor Madelaine,' she sympathized softly, knowing that the other woman's heart was in the right place, even if somewhat misguided on occasion.

Beau Garrett gave a snort of dismissal. 'You're obviously a local too, so I'll ask you the same question I've been asking all evening—the only reason I'm here at all! The garden at The Old Vicarage is a mess; who do you know who could do something with it?'

She gave a faint smile. 'What answers have you already received?'

'"Jaz Logan, old boy",' he mimicked. '"Unorthodox but brilliant".'

'The major.' She nodded.

'"Jaz turned the chaos of my garden into wonderfully manageable order",' he mimicked again, just as distinctively.

'That was Barbara Scott from the village shop,' she guessed.

'"Jaz is an absolute *treasure*".'

'Betty Booth, the vicar's wife.'

'And according to our hostess, "Jaz is a darling",' he finished with some disgust.

She gave a throaty chuckle. 'Good for Madelaine.'

'No, wait a minute, I think I got that quote slightly wrong,' Beau Garrett corrected harshly. 'What she actually said was, "Jaz made something beautiful of my darling little garden".'

She chuckled again; only Madelaine, bless her, could possibly describe the acre of land that surrounded this grand old house as a 'darling little garden'.

'So what appears to be the problem with the advice you've already been given?' she prompted interestedly.

'My "problem", as you call it, is that this Jaz Logan sounds slightly effeminate to me,' Beau Garrett bit out tersely. 'The last thing I want is the Old English village cliché, masses of beds of pink flowers and roses around the door!'

'Tell me, Mr Garrett—' she turned to him frowningly in the darkness '—if you have so much contempt for village life, why on earth have you moved here?'

'Surely that's obvious?' he rasped, at the same time turning so that the moonlight shone fully on the right side of his face, throwing into stark relief the livid scar that ran from brow to jaw, a lasting souvenir from the car accident that had almost killed him four months ago.

She would be lying if she didn't inwardly acknowledge she was deeply shocked by the thought of the injury he had suffered to have received such a scar, but she forced her own expression to remain unemotional as she looked at it. She had a feeling, from the bitterness that edged everything he said, that the scars inside this man were much more destructive than the more obvious one on his face.

'Not particularly,' she shrugged dismissively. 'Scars fade, Mr Garrett,' she added gently.

'So I've been told,' he said bitterly. *But not soon enough for him,* his tone implied.

She looked up at him consideringly. 'Tell me, Mr Garrett, have you ever lived in a village before?'

His gaze narrowed guardedly. 'No…'

'I thought not,' she nodded. 'Well, we're a curious lot,' she warned from experience. 'If it's "peace and quiet" you're looking for, then you've come to the wrong place,' she told him ruefully.

Beau Garrett moved suddenly, swinging violently away from her, his face once more in shadow. 'I have no intention of satisfying anyone's curiosity.' The last word came out with suppressed scorn.

'I wish you luck,' she said quietly.

He became very still in the darkness, that very stillness all the more ominous because of his earlier impatience. 'What's that supposed to mean?'

'Nothing really.' She shrugged. 'Except…'

'Except?' he prompted harshly.

She gave another shrug. 'What people don't know they will simply make up.' And she should know!

He gave a scornful snort as he walked over to the door. 'Let them!'

'Oh, they will,' she assured him softly, remaining on the terrace as he let himself back into the noisily crowded house, with the obvious intention of making his excuses and leaving.

But if Beau Garrett thought he had seen the last of her, either, then he was sadly mistaken.

CHAPTER TWO

'WHY didn't you tell me when we met at Madelaine's on Friday evening that you work for Jaz Logan?'

She looked up from the bills scattered across the desk in the less-than-tidy room that passed as an office at the garden centre, completely unsurprised that Beau Garrett was the first customer of this less-than-busy Monday morning. In fact, she had been expecting him...

She shrugged. 'You didn't ask.'

Irritation twisted the scar on his face. 'I don't suppose I did. But I would have thought, as I actually asked you about the man, that you might have volunteered the information,' he added accusingly.

She grinned unabashedly as she sat back in her chair. 'Something else you should know about village life; we're always curious to know about others, but rarely volunteer information about ourselves. Anyway,' she added determinedly as he would have spoken, 'it's actually worse than you thought.' She stood up, wiping a dirt-smeared hand down her worn denims. 'You see, I don't work for Jaz Logan—I am Jaz Logan.' She held her hand out in formal greeting.

Beau Garrett made no effort to take that proffered hand. Instead his silver-grey gaze moved over her with deliberate slowness, from her muddy wellington boots pushed into dirty denims, her over-large blue jumper, ragged at the sleeve ends, with a hole in one elbow, that critical gaze finally coming to rest on her face and the

10

long ebony hair that had been blown about earlier by the strong wind blowing as she worked outside.

Despite hours spent outside in all weather, her skin remained creamy magnolia, her chin determinedly pointed, mouth wide and smiling, her nose small and snub above the fuller top lip, deep blue eyes fringed by lashes as dark as her hair, the latter worn long and in a shaggily unkempt style—it looked like that most of the time anyway, so Jaz just left it that way!

'"Unorthodox but brilliant",' Beau Garrett murmured derisively. 'I take it by that remark that the major meant it's unusual to find a female landscape gardener?'

Jaz smiled. 'The major is a little old-fashioned,' she excused, not in the least offended by the remark.

'"Capable of turning chaos into order",' Beau Garrett continued dryly.

She shrugged. 'If you happen to frequent the well-stocked village shop, you'll see that Barbara is something of a perfectionist when it comes to order.' Even the cans of soup daren't be out of line on her shelves!

'"An absolute treasure",' he derided.

Jaz nodded. 'Betty never has a bad word to say about anyone. But don't forget the "darling" remark,' she reminded him cheerily.

He didn't look impressed by her own recall of their conversation on Friday evening, in fact that dark scowl was back on those mesmerizingly handsome features.

Maybe she should have told him who she was the other evening, but at the time it had been interesting hearing other people's opinions of her without the inhibition of knowing she was the one being discussed. Although she didn't somehow think Beau Garrett would be too impressed with that excuse!

Seen in the clear light of day like this, that scar on

his face was much more noticeable, a livid red mark against the otherwise paleness of his skin. Not that the scar detracted from his attractiveness in the least, he just looked even more dangerously piratical.

Although from the challenging glitter in those silver-grey eyes she had a feeling Beau Garrett wouldn't appreciate being told of that particular observation!

But that scar apart, he had to be one of the most handsome men ever to grace the small screen; aged in his late thirties, possibly early forties, well over six feet in height, lithely masculine, the slightly overlong dark hair flecked with grey at his temples, his chin square and determined in the bold handsomeness of his face.

Was it any wonder that Madelaine, only forty-five herself but widowed for the last eight years, had been eager to invite him over for drinks; not only had it been a feather in the other woman's cap to be the first in the village to socially entertain the celebrity who had decided to appear in their midst, but Beau Garrett had to be the likeliest husband material to appear in the village for some time. If ever!

Not being a great fan of television, or those gossipy magazines that seemed so popular nowadays, Jaz had no idea whether or not this man was married. But one thing she did know just from looking at him; those lines of bitterness beside his eyes and mouth didn't auger well for any woman showing a matrimonial interest in him.

Thank goodness Jaz didn't count herself amongst that number. She was far too busy keeping her garden centre and landscape gardening business going to have any time for love herself, let alone a husband and children.

'"Jaz"?' Beau Garrett finally prompted dryly.

Her mouth tightened, her cheeks flushing slightly.

'Short for Jasmina,' she said with disgust. 'Although I wouldn't advise you to ever call me that,' she added tersely. 'The last person who did still has the bruises to prove it!'

Humour softened the harshness of his features. 'I feel the same way about Beauregard.' He grimaced. 'Parents have a lot to answer for, don't they, when it comes to the choice of names for their poor, unsuspecting children?'

They certainly did—and Jaz wasn't sure she didn't feel more sorry for him than she did herself. Beauregard, for goodness' sake!

She nodded. 'If I ever have a child of my own I'm going to call it either Mary, if it's a girl, or Mark, if it's a boy—if only because there's absolutely nothing you can do with plain, solid names like that!'

Beau Garrett frowned. 'I couldn't help noticing that it says "J Logan and Sons" on the sign outside the garden centre?'

'My father,' she supplied abruptly. 'His name was John. But there aren't any sons. Just me,' she eyed him challengingly. 'The "and sons" was my father's idea of a joke.'

'I see,' he murmured, obviously not seeing at all. 'You said "was"?' He looked at her with narrowed eyes.

She gave a brief inclination of her head; for someone not brought up in a village, this man was doing a very good job of extracting information himself! 'My father died three years ago when I was twenty-two and fresh out of college. I just left the sign up because—well, because it's always been there,' she finished lamely, but knowing that wasn't really the reason she had left the sign as it was.

It served as a reminder. Of what, she wasn't quite sure. But one thing she did know, every time she looked at that sign she felt a new resolve to make a success of this gardening centre.

'And your mother?' Beau Garrett prompted softly.

Her mouth twisted humourlessly. 'I don't think she appreciated the joke, either—she walked out on my father and me when I was just seventeen!'

'I'm sorry,' he bit out abruptly.

'Oh, don't be,' Jaz dismissed hardly, moving to sit back behind her desk. She had no intention of telling him that her mother hadn't left alone. Or that she and her lover had been killed in a car accident in the South of France three months later. 'You know, Mr Garrett—' she looked up at him assessingly '—you're very good at this. No wonder your television show is so successful if you get your guests to talk about themselves in this same candid way!' She hadn't discussed her mother, or the fact that she had left her father and herself, for longer than she could remember, and yet a few minutes into conversation with this man and she seemed to have told him half her life history!

But if she didn't want to pursue that subject any further, then Beau Garrett seemed to share her view, his expression having tightened bleakly, his eyes glittering silver. 'Perhaps we should get back to the subject in hand,' he rasped. 'You already know the problem, the question is, do you have the time to do something with the wildness of The Old Vicarage garden?'

'Of course.' Her own tone matched his in crispness, determined to get this conversation back on the footing of two strangers discussing a business transaction. 'Would you like me to call round this afternoon and give you a quote on time and cost?'

He arched dark brows. 'Don't you have to check your diary or anything like that first?'

She met his gaze unblinkingly. 'No.'

Those brows rose higher. 'Or need to know exactly what work I want done?'

Her mouth twisted wryly. 'I thought we could discuss that when I call round this afternoon.'

The mocking humour returned to those pale grey eyes. 'Business a little slow at the moment, is it?' he drawled dryly.

In truth, business, in the middle of March, was almost non-existent!

It was too early in the season for any of her regulars to need their lawns or flower-beds tended, and the flowers and plants she had been carefully nurturing in the greenhouses. To add to that, she had nothing in the books for the landscape gardening side of the business. In fact, if she managed to get a down payment from Beau Garrett for the work he wanted done, she might actually be able to pay off one or two of the bills that were piling up on her desk!

'A little,' she allowed lightly. 'But, then, it always is in March,' she defended dismissively. 'Although it's the perfect time of year to clear and landscape a garden,' she added reassuringly.

His mouth twisted mockingly. 'I believe you.'

Jaz gave him a considering look. 'I can't believe you've really bought The Old Vicarage.'

When the 'Sold' sign had gone up outside the old house a month ago everyone in the village had been agog with curiosity as to who could possibly have bought such a monstrosity. The house itself was big and old, very run-down, had stood empty for the last five years since the last people to rent it had moved out into one of the more convenient cottages on the edge of the village, claiming that the house was too big and draughty to keep warm, that the roof leaked, and the electric wiring and drainage systems were antiquated to say the least.

Beau Garrett eyed Jaz speculatively now. 'Is there some reason why I shouldn't have done?'

All of the above, Jaz would have thought.

'It's very run-down,' she began tentatively.

'The builder started work on that this morning,' he dismissed.

Next!, his tone seemed to imply.

'I would have thought it was very inconvenient for commuting to London,' Jaz obliged.

This man's chat show had taken the prime-time ten o'clock spot on a Friday evening for the last ten years, mainly because of his decisive, informative interviews, but his dark, brooding good looks certainly hadn't done him any harm, either. But the village was a couple of hundred miles away from London, hardly within commuting distance for a man who worked from a London studio.

'Good,' came his uncompromising answer, his silver gaze palely challenging, his mouth thinning grimly.

Jaz shrugged. 'Isn't it also a little big for just one man to live in? Unless, of course, you intend bringing your family up here, too,' she added as an afterthought. After all, two could play at this game...

'I don't,' he answered unhelpfully. 'Now could we get back to the subject of your working on the vicarage garden?' It was made as a request, but the steely edge to his tone clearly told Jaz that he had no intention of discussing his private life with her. Or, indeed, with anyone else!

That was fine with her; it was his private life, after all.

She nodded. 'Well, as I've said, I'll call round this afternoon and we can discuss what needs to be done. After that, I can probably start working on it by—would Wednesday morning be okay with you?'

'Fine,' he agreed tersely, turning to leave, and then pausing as he reached the door. 'I hope you're going to be more reliable than the builder—he should have started work a week ago!'

'And he arrived this morning,' Jaz said admiringly. 'That's pretty good. You must have made a good impression on him.'

Beau Garrett's mouth twisted ruefully. 'No—I just made a damned nuisance of myself by telephoning every day for the last week to find out when he was going to start work!'

She laughed, standing up. 'Maybe village life is going to suit you, after all, Mr Garrett,' she said appreciatively. 'You obviously know how to deal with unreliable workmen,' she explained at his questioning look.

'Knowing how to deal with them has nothing to do with it,' he bit out dismissively. 'I just don't suffer fools gladly.'

Now that, even on such brief acquaintance, she could believe!

But even so, Dennis Davis, the only builder for miles around, was well known for his lackadaisical attitude to turning up for jobs on time—in fact, Jaz had been waiting for weeks herself for Dennis to fix a leak on one of her shed roofs!

She grinned sympathetically. 'I can assure you, Mr

Garrett, that if I say I'll be with you at two-thirty this afternoon, then that's exactly when I will be there.'

'Call me Beau,' he invited abruptly.

Jaz felt the warm colour enter her cheeks, not sure she could take such a liberty—even when invited to do so—by this national television figure; it somehow seemed far too familiar with this distantly haughty man.

'Jaz,' she returned uncomfortably. 'Two-thirty, then,' she added briskly.

'Fine,' he accepted tersely. 'I'm out of coffee, so I thought I might call in at the village shop on the way home,' he added dryly, that hint of humour once again in those silver eyes. 'But I should have escaped by two-thirty.'

Effectively telling Jaz that as well as being aware of the neat precision with which Barbara Scott liked to stack her shelves, she was also, predictably, the biggest gossip in the village; there was no way Barbara would easily relinquish the novelty of Beau Garrett's presence in her shop!

Jaz smiled appreciatively. 'You may just get used to village life, after all!'

'Somehow I'm starting to doubt that,' he rasped dismissively.

Jaz stood at the doorway watching him as he strode purposefully to the black Range Rover parked in the muddy driveway, raising a hand in farewell as he drove away.

But Jaz's smile faded as soon as he had gone, a frown marring her creamy brow as she returned to the problem of the pile of bills on her desk even while her thoughts actually remained on Beau Garrett's last comment.

'Somehow' she very much doubted he would 'get used to village life', either.

Which posed the question: what was he doing here in the first place?

CHAPTER THREE

'I'M SO sorry I'm late!' Jaz burst out flusteredly as soon as Beau Garrett opened the door to The Old Vicarage in answer to her ring on the bell. 'I did start out in good time to arrive at two-thirty, but the van developed a puncture on the drive here, and I had to stop and exchange it for the spare wheel, and then—'

'Slow down, Jaz,' he cut in mildly. 'And calm down, too,' he advised with a sweeping glance over her flushed face. 'You have dirt on your cheek,' he added softly.

She raised an impatient hand to rub the spot where she thought the dirt might be.

'The other cheek,' he told her ruefully. 'Look, come inside,' he added impatiently before she could transfer her attention to the other side of her face. 'The washroom is through that door there.' He pointed to the left of the front door. 'The kitchen is at the other end of this hallway. Come through when you're ready,' he said dryly.

This would have to happen to her today, Jaz fumed as she went to the washroom and scrubbed the dirt impatiently from her cheek, and after assurances earlier to Beau Garrett that he could rely on her to be on time!

She had been just half a mile away from The Old Vicarage when she realized the van wasn't responding properly, that it certainly wasn't going where she was steering it, pulling in to the side of the road to get out and discover that one of her front tyres was absolutely flat.

The spare wheel didn't look much better, but at least it wasn't flat, although it had taken some time to get the punctured wheel off the van, the vehicle so old all the bolts seemed to have rusted up. And, as she had never changed a wheel in her life before...

Although none of that changed the fact that she had arrived at Beau Garrett's home half an hour later than she had assured him she would.

'I really am sorry I'm late,' she apologized again as she entered the kitchen a few minutes later, coming to an abrupt halt in the doorway as she looked around the transformed kitchen.

The last time she had seen this large room it had been as old and run down as the rest of the house, cracked lino on the floor, the kitchen cupboards of a particularly unattractive shade of grey, as had been the tiles on the walls, the work surfaces a depressing black, the range that provided heat as well as cooking facilities, old and temperamental.

The lino had been replaced by mellow-coloured flagstones, the kitchen units now a light oak, the kitchen tiles a bright sunny yellow, the new Aga an attractive cream, and—thankfully!—throwing out lots of heat.

'Wow,' she murmured appreciatively. 'This looks really great.'

He turned from pouring coffee into two mugs. 'There was no way I could have moved in here with the kitchen the way that it was,' he dismissed, putting the mugs, cream, and sugar down on the kitchen table before indicating for her to join him in sitting down.

Jaz sat, some of her earlier flusteredness starting to fade in the warm relaxation of the transformed room. 'I don't blame you,' she nodded, adding cream to her mug. 'It always was a cold, uninviting room.' She took a grateful sip of her unsweetened coffee.

'Always…?' Beau Garrett repeated softly as he sat in the chair opposite.

Jaz looked up sharply; this man didn't miss much, did he? She really would have to start remembering that!

'Hmm.' She gave a rueful sigh. 'I may as well tell you before someone else does; my grandfather was the last vicar to actually live in this house. The man who took over from him moved into the new vicarage at the other end of the village where the Booths now live. But I spent a lot of time here as a child,' she added flatly.

'I see,' Beau Garrett murmured slowly.

Jaz met his gaze unwaveringly. 'Do you?'

'Not really.' He grimaced. 'But if I live here long enough I'm sure that one way or another I'll get to hear most of the local gossip,' he added with distaste.

She was sure he would too. One way or another.

'How did your visit to the shop go this morning?' she changed the subject abruptly.

He gave a rueful smile. 'Pretty much as predicted. Although, thankfully, I was saved after about fifteen minutes of fending off Mrs Scott's increasingly personal questions by the arrival of another customer!'

Jaz nodded, smiling. 'At which time you gratefully beat a hasty retreat.'

'Very hasty,' he confirmed grimly.

'I shouldn't worry about it too much,' Jaz advised lightly. 'Once you've lived here twenty years or so they'll lose interest!'

'Oh wonderful!' he said with feeling. 'Somehow village life isn't quite as I imagined it would be.' He gave a disgusted shake of his head.

'Birds twittering in the hedgerows, children playing happily on the village green, neighbours chatting happily to each other over the garden fences?' Jaz guessed teasingly.

'Something like that,' he confirmed dryly.

'Oh, it can be like that,' Jaz assured him. 'Not usually in March, though. Too cold,' she grinned. 'And beneath the birds twittering, the happy children playing, neighbours chatting, you'll find there is always the underlying gossip that binds us all together.'

'The latter I can quite well do without,' Beau Garrett assured her hardly.

She shrugged. 'I did try to warn you the other evening.'

'A little late, wouldn't you say, when I've obviously already purchased The Old Vicarage?' he drawled.

'Just a little,' she conceded ruefully. 'But, don't worry, if you intend staying, you'll soon get used to it.'

'Oh I intend staying,' he told her flatly. 'But I intend living here in quiet seclusion, have no intention of doing anything that will give the villagers cause to gossip about me,' he added grimly.

Perhaps now wasn't the time to tell him that he wouldn't actually need to do anything to be the subject of gossip; just his being here at all, a well-known television star, had the inhabitants of Aberton agog with speculation as to why he had bought a house here. The last Jaz had heard, from the postman this morning as he handed her her letters, Beau Garrett had come to the village to escape an unhappy love affair when the woman in his life left him following the car accident that had left his face scarred.

That may be true, Jaz really had no idea, but somehow she doubted it was any more accurate than the rumour that he was here to research a book! What sort of book, and what sort of research, she couldn't imagine, having heard from Beau Garret himself of his desire to be left in peace and solitude, but she had no intention of adding fuel to that particular fire by confiding that knowledge with anyone else, her answers to the postman noncommittal to say the least.

'Perhaps we should go and look at the garden now?' she suggested briskly, deciding enough had already been said concerning the speculation about him in the village.

'The jungle, I call it.' He stood up. 'Although I am hoping that one day I'll be able to call it a garden,' he added wryly as they walked outside.

He was right, it *was* more like a jungle, Jaz realized with a heavy heart, years of rubbish accumulated in grass that was thigh high, overgrown with weeds, several of the trees in need of cutting down completely, and the greenhouse, once so lovingly tended by her grandmother, almost falling down, every pane of glass broken.

Looking at it Jaz couldn't help remembering how in previous years she had played in this garden, built dens in the bushes, eaten picnics with her grandparents on the smooth green lawn, sat on the swing beneath the apple tree dreaming of a time when she would have her own home, her own apple tree with its swing, and children laughing as they played on it.

Now, at twenty-five, she had come to believe those dreams would never be more than that...

'A disaster, isn't it?' Beau Garrett rasped disgustedly.

Jaz gave herself a mental shake; she was here to do

a job, not wallow in the past. 'Not really,' she assured him crisply. 'I'll need to clear all the rubbish before we can actually begin putting it in any order, but I think most of it is salvageable.'

'You have more optimism than I do, then,' he dismissed with a shake of his head. 'Sometimes I wonder what on earth I thought I was doing taking on a place like this!' he muttered almost to himself.

Jaz turned to look at him. 'Searching for your own piece of paradise?' she suggested huskily, knowing that being back here again, after all these years, had affected her more deeply than she cared to admit. 'My grandfather always said that you have to find contentment inside yourself before you can appreciate any other happiness in your life.' And she had known all about discontent...

'Did he really?' Beau Garrett rasped harshly, his aloofness of Friday evening returning with a vengeance as he looked down his arrogant nose at her.

Jaz turned away, her cheeks flushed as she realized she had stepped over some imaginary line. 'I'm sorry. I shouldn't have—I wasn't necessarily referring to you,' she finished lamely, knowing it was being at The Old Vicarage again, her own memories, that had prompted the comment. And it hadn't been directed at Beau Garrett at all, but at herself...

'It doesn't matter.' He turned away abruptly. 'Are you still available to start on Wednesday morning?'

'Yes, of course—'

'Then consider yourself hired,' he bit out curtly. 'Now, if you wouldn't mind...? I have some other things I need to do this afternoon.'

Jaz didn't 'mind' at all, felt an overwhelming urge to

get away herself, had reminisced quite enough for one afternoon, thank you!

'You'll need a quote for how much the work is going to cost—'

'Just do it,' he rasped, obviously impatient for this conversation to be over now. 'And send me the bill.'

'Er...' She grimaced, too embarrassed now to quite be able to meet that silvery gaze. 'I'll need to have a skip delivered to take away all the rubbish, and then there's—'

'Jaz, if you need a deposit to cover those costs then why don't you just ask for one?' Beau Garrett cut in impatiently.

'Because I hate asking people for money, that's why!' She felt stung into replying, glaring up at him, all her earlier feelings of sympathy towards him evaporating in the face of his arrogant rudeness.

'Then it's no wonder that the tyres on your van are so bald they develop punctures, your business is obviously falling down around your ears, and the clothes you're wearing would make a scarecrow look well dressed!' he came back scathingly before striding back into the kitchen.

Jaz stared after him, too stunned by the suddenness of the attack to find an immediate reply.

The fact that every word he spoke was the truth certainly didn't help!

The van *was* old, left to her on her father's death, as was the run-down garden centre. As for her clothes... she couldn't remember when she had last been able to afford anything new.

But for Beau Garrett to have said those things to her...!

'I'm sorry,' he spoke softly behind.

Jaz had stiffened at the first sound of his voice, blinking back the tears now, determined he shouldn't see that he had made her cry with the hurtful things he had said to her.

'Jaz—'

'No need to apologize for telling the truth,' she assured brightly as she turned to face him, blue eyes not quite meeting those probing silver ones.

He shook his head, his sigh heavy. 'I'm a little—I shouldn't have taken out my bad temper on you,' he rasped with a self-disgusted shake of his head.

Jaz moistened dry lips before speaking. 'Perhaps I shouldn't have spoken so personally to you, either.' She grimaced. 'It's this place. I—' she sighed, her frown pained. 'I'd forgotten.'

'Forgotten what?' Beau Garrett looked at her compellingly.

Jaz found herself caught and held by the intensity of that silvery gaze, feeling a little like a rabbit must do when caught in the glare of a car's headlights; trapped, mesmerized, totally unable to move.

But at the same time her own instinct for privacy came to the fore, giving her the impetus to break that gaze even as she gave a dismissive laugh. 'Nothing of any importance,' she assured him lightly.

He looked for a brief minute as if he would like to argue that point, but as Jaz continued to look at him unblinkingly he finally gave a rueful shrug. 'Here.' He held a cheque out to her. 'That should cover any initial expenses you may have.'

A glance at the amount written on the cheque he gave her told Jaz that it would probably cover the cost of all of the work to be done here, not just the initial expenses.

Pride warred with necessity inside her—and it was

necessity that finally won out. After all, she would do the work, and it would probably cost as much as this, so it wasn't as if she were taking the money under false pretences. Besides, accepting it would mean that, as well as being able to pay off most of the more pressing bills, for a change she would also be able to eat more than either baked beans, or tomatoes, on toast!

The thought of a nice roast chicken for her dinner was enough to make her mouth water. And her pride seem petty.

'Thank you,' she accepted huskily as she stuffed the cheque into her denims pocket. 'Eight o'clock on Wednesday morning, then.'

He winced as the sound of banging could be heard from the front of the house, Dennis still in the process of putting up the scaffolding in preparation of repairing the roof when Jaz arrived a short time ago. 'Make it nine o'clock,' Beau Garrett suggested. 'If the place is going to be like a building site for the foreseeable future, I might as well arrange it so that I have some peace in the mornings, at least until after nine o'clock!'

Having accepted and been present at Madelaine's drinks party last Friday, peace was something Jaz didn't think this man was going to find too much of in the immediate future. Every other hostess in the village, from Barbara Scott at the shop to Betty Booth, the pretty young wife of the vicar, was going to be inviting him to lunch or dinner. Invitations, if he didn't want to cause offence, he would find it hard to refuse, having accepted Madelaine's.

Although somehow Jaz didn't think Beau Garrett particularly cared whether or not he offended people!

Oh, well, that was his problem. Her own, more immediate concern was cashing his cheque so that she might have some money herself for a change.

'That's fine with me,' she agreed lightly, hesitating as she turned to leave. 'I should keep an eye on Dennis, if I were you,' she added with a rueful grimace. 'He has a habit of setting up the scaffolding and then forgetting to come back to start the job.'

Beau Garrett's mouth set in a grim line. 'Not this one, he won't.'

No, he probably wouldn't, Jaz conceded inwardly as she went back out to her van. Even work-shy Dennis must have already realized that Beau Garrett wasn't a man to cross.

Something she had better remember herself if she wanted to keep her own job at The Old Vicarage.

If only just being here didn't bring back such vivid memories for her. Memories she would much rather forget.

CHAPTER FOUR

'WHAT the hell do you think you're doing?'

Jaz turned frowningly at the sound of Beau Garrett's furious voice, struggling to hold a rather large rock in her arms as she did so. 'Sorry?' The wind was strong this morning, whipping her hair into her face and eyes, so that she looked at him through the screen of her tousled hair as he strode purposefully down the garden towards her.

'I said,' he grated much closer to her, reaching out to take the rock from her arms and drop it disgustedly into the wheelbarrow beside them, 'what do you think you're doing?' His eyes glittered silver as Jaz was finally able to brush the hair from her eyes and look at him.

And then wished she hadn't.

Not that he wasn't worth looking at, virilely attractive in faded denims and a navy-blue sweater to keep out the cold. But the anger she could see in his face, that scar shown in stark relief, were enough to make her take a step backwards.

She moistened wind-dry lips. 'Don't worry, I'm not throwing these rocks away—'

'I don't care if you smash them to pieces and scatter them to the wind,' he cut in harshly. 'What I want to know is why you're picking them up in the first place!'

Jaz's apprehension at his obvious anger turned to confusion. 'Exactly what I told you I would do,' she answered slowly. 'Clearing away all the debris so that I can see what we have to work with.'

She had arrived at The Old Vicarage just over an hour ago, Beau Garrett obviously out when she'd got there: his Range Rover had been missing from the driveway, and there had been no answer to the ringing of the doorbell, only Dennis up on the roof industriously hammering away.

So Jaz had simply let herself into the garden by the side gate, had already half filled the skip at the side of the house that had been delivered yesterday, with old bicycles and other rubbish that had no practical use. In fact, she couldn't imagine how an old bath could possibly have found its way amongst the weeds; as far as she was aware, apart from the kitchen, Beau Garrett hadn't yet started on the redecorating of the other rooms in the house. But she had dumped that into the skip along with the other accumulating rubbish.

Beau Garrett's expression was darkly disapproving. 'I presumed when we agreed that you would do the work that you would have someone to help you.'

Jaz raised dark brows. 'Such as?'

'Such as a labourer of some kind to do the heavy work,' he bit out impatiently.

'Ah.' Jaz straightened knowingly, realizing that her five feet four inches in height were far from imposing. 'A man, you mean?'

'Well, of course I mean a man,' he came back with barely constrained irritation. 'I had no idea that you intended doing all this heavy work yourself.'

'Mr Garrett—'

'Beau,' he snapped.

'Beau,' she complied with a nod. 'Apart from old

Fred at the garden centre, I don't have anyone working for me. I'm a one-man band—'

'One-woman band,' he corrected grimly.

'And that's the problem,' she guessed ruefully.

'Of course that's the problem!' he snapped. 'I can't possibly allow you to collect all this rubbish up and carry it out to the skip—'

'I'm using a wheelbarrow,' she pointed out practically.

'Wheeling it out to the skip, then,' he corrected with no show of a lessening of his impatience.

She gave him a reassuring smile. 'I realize I'm not very big, but I'm really quite strong, you know.'

His gaze raked over her scathingly, obviously not at all impressed with her height or her size-ten frame. 'You may be,' he allowed skeptically. 'But there's no way I'm going to let you clear all this lot on your own.' He made a sweeping gesture that encompassed all the rubbish still scattered about the weed-engulfed garden.

And there was no way that Jaz was going to use some of the precious money he had given her in order to hire a labourer for a couple of days to help with the clearance! Especially when she knew she was perfectly capable of doing it herself.

'I'll help you,' Beau told her dryly as he seemed to read at least some of her thoughts.

But hopefully he couldn't read the ones she was having now!

Beau Garrett, television star, urbanely elegant man, always voted in the top five in the 'sexiest men on television' poll that came out each year, was going to shift stones and debris like some common labourer?

Worse—he was going to shift stones and debris like a common labourer alongside her!

She may have given up any interest in love and marriage, but that didn't mean she was immune to men, that she couldn't be totally aware of one in a sexual way. As she was totally aware of Beau Garrett...

Top five 'sexiest men on television' be damned—this man was too lethally attractive for his own—or anyone else's!—good.

She shook her head. 'I don't think that's a good idea—'

'Why not?' he rasped impatiently.

Jaz had no intention of telling him the real reason 'why not'; the truth being that, dressed in disreputable denims and a ragged sweater, her face hot and sweaty from lifting heavy weights, she felt about as feminine as one of the rusted bicycles she had thrown in the skip!

Not that she thought a man like Beau Garrett would have looked at her twice even if she were looking her best, but she still had her pride, even if he did think she made 'a scarecrow look well dressed'.

No matter how determined she may have been on Monday afternoon not to let him see how hurt she had been by that insulting remark, it had definitely hit a raw nerve...

She shrugged. 'My insurance wouldn't cover any injuries you—'

'Insurance be damned,' Beau Garrett cut in scathingly. 'This is my garden, and as such my rubbish, and if I choose to help clear it away then that's my problem, not yours.'

Jaz could clearly see the challenge in his gaze. 'I'm not sure an insurance company would see it quite that way—' She broke off, knowing her protests to be completely wasted as he moved determinedly to pick up one of the larger stones that littered this particular corner of the garden.

'Where could all these rocks have come from?' he muttered disgustedly as he dumped it into the wheel-barrow.

'My grandmother's rock garden...?' she suggested with a grimace.

'I should have guessed!' Beau shot her a rueful glance as he continued to load the rocks into the barrow.

'Mmm,' Jaz nodded, blue eyes glittering mischievously. 'She was very fond of her rock garden.'

He paused before bending to pick up another rock, one dark brow raised over mocking grey eyes. 'Are you going to help or just stand there watching me all day?'

Her cheeks warmed with embarrassment. 'Sorry. I—I just can't believe you're actually doing this.' She gave a dazed shake of her head even as she moved to pick up one of the smaller rocks.

'Believe it,' he muttered through clenched teeth as he dumped another huge rock none-too-gently on top of the others. 'Besides...' he straightened, running his hands down his denim-clad thighs to remove the dirt '...you don't seriously think, now that I've seen you're managing here alone, that I could just calmly go back into the house and read the newspaper, do you?' His expression was grim.

Jaz gave a shrug. 'You could always try pretending that you hadn't seen me.'

'No,' he bit out, 'I couldn't.' A frown furrowed his brow as he looked down at all the rocks still remaining on the ground. 'If we put all these in the skip there won't be any room for anything else.'

'Oh, but they aren't going in the skip,' she assured him happily.

His frown deepened. 'In that case, what do you intend doing with them?'

'Don't worry.' She laughed. 'I'm not the sort to steal them to use for another job!'

Beau gave a disgusted shake of his head. 'I didn't for a moment think that you were!'

Jaz grinned. 'Then, in answer to your question, I'm going to store them in the greenhouse.'

He gave a grimace. 'The last time I looked in there it was full of cigarette butts and empty beer cans; I think some of the local kids have been using it to hold small parties!'

'Already disposed of in the skip,' she assured him, prevented from wheeling the barrow over the garden to the greenhouse as Beau neatly took over the handles.

'And exactly why are we keeping these particular rocks?' he prompted impatiently, barely breathing hard from the effort of lifting the heavy weight across the garden.

'So that I can eventually make another rock garden.' Jaz studiously ignored his disapproving frown as she helped transfer the rocks to the greenhouse. It was what he was paying her for, after all!

'Right,' he acknowledged self-derisively.

They worked in companionable silence, after that. Well…as companionable as it could be for Jaz when she was aware of everything about him, from his tousled dark hair, lithe body, to the long muscular length of his legs.

If anyone had told her a week ago that she would be working alongside Beau Garrett, of all people, she would have laughed in their faces!

'Time for a coffee break, I think,' he decided crisply

ten minutes later when the rocks were neatly stacked in the greenhouse.

'Oh, but—' She broke off her protest as he looked at her down the length of that arrogant nose. No doubt that look had as equal success in silencing the guests on his television programme!

'Coffee break. Now. In the house,' he bit out succinctly.

She quirked dark brows derisively. 'Will Dennis be joining us too?'

Beau's mouth twisted scathingly. 'Hardly.'

She shook her head. 'Then you have no need to worry about me, either. I brought a flask of coffee with me in the van,' she assured him.

And then felt totally embarrassed by the admission. Although why she should do so she had no idea; she always took a flask of coffee and a packed lunch when she was off working for the day. And thanks to Beau Garrett's cheque she had been able to put something a little more interesting than jam in the sandwiches!

'Save it for later,' he dismissed uninterestedly, not waiting for her reply before striding off towards the house.

Because he was used to being listened to and obeyed, Jaz guessed ruefully as she trailed along reluctantly behind him. She was afraid he would have to get used to a much slower response if he intended remaining in Aberton.

Although not this time, Jaz allowed self-derisively, feeling slightly guilty as she could still hear Dennis working up on the roof, but quite happy to drink a cup of coffee herself if it was the same brew Beau had made for her on Monday.

It was, its delicious aroma quickly filling the warmth

of the kitchen. Jaz crossed the room with sock-covered feet to sit at the table, having left her muddy boots outside on the step.

'Mmm, that smells good,' she accepted gratefully as Beau placed the steaming mug on the table in front of her. 'Er—I wasn't being rude before when I made that remark about you shifting the rocks,' she began awkwardly. 'It's just that the last time I saw you it was on public television, interviewing Catherine what's-her-name, the Oscar-winner.'

He stiffened, his expression bleak, his eyes glittering hardly. 'A beautiful lady,' he allowed tightly as he moved away to get his own coffee.

'Very.' Jaz nodded, frowning as he kept the rigidness of his back turned towards her.

She hadn't intended to annoy him by mentioning his television programme—although from his suddenly frosty manner that's obviously what she had succeeded in doing!

'Mr—Beau,' she amended as he turned that silver glare on her. 'I'm sorry if I—'

'Life is going to become extremely tedious over the next few weeks if you keep apologizing every ten minutes!' he bit out tautly, a humourless smile curving his lips as he looked at her challengingly.

Once again Jaz felt the embarrassed colour in her cheeks. Even if she was completely aware that Beau Garrett had deliberately turned the tables on her...

Beau was giving her a considering look now, further enhancing that blush in her cheeks. 'You have a look of Catherine yourself, you know,' he finally murmured slowly.

'Yeah—right!' She came back with the same scornful

comment she had heard from a friend's teenage son a couple of weeks ago.

Although her smile wavered, and then disappeared completely as she found no answering humour in Beau Garrett's face.

She continued to frown at him for several long minutes, and Beau silently returned the steadiness of her gaze. 'You were just trying to change the subject,' she finally accused dryly.

'True,' he acknowledged unabashedly—nothing in his expression to confirm or deny his reference to her resembling the beautiful actress.

Not that Jaz had taken him seriously for a moment; with her wild dark hair and make-upless face, her clothes ready for the ragbag, she bore absolutely no resemblance to the beautifully elegant actress who appeared so strikingly on the big screen. It had merely been said as a ploy to distract her from her remark concerning Beau's television programme.

Although she still had no idea what the problem was with her mentioning something that was obviously so successful…

She sighed heavily. 'I think the Catherine Zeta-Jones remark was a little mean of you,' she grimaced.

'Coffee break over,' Beau decided abruptly. 'And I wasn't being in the least ''mean'' with the Catherine Z J remark,' he added mockingly, that rapier-sharp gaze narrowed on her flushed face now. 'It's your mouth, I think,' he said slowly—just when Jaz had decided she really couldn't stand his all-seeing scrutiny a moment longer! 'The top lip is a perfect bow, the bottom lip sensuously full.'

A perfect bow…? Sensuously full…!

Her next movement was purely instinctive, her

tongue moving moistly across that perfect bow and sensuously full bottom lip, her breath catching in her throat as she saw that Beau Garrett's gaze was riveted on the movement.

She may be twenty-five in years, but in experience she was a mere babe-in-arms. Especially where a man of Beau Garrett's charisma was concerned! There had been few dates in her teen years, even fewer in her twenties, and she couldn't remember anyone who had ever looked at her with such frankly male appraisal. It wasn't comfortable.

She gave a dismissive shake of her head. 'I think you need to get your eyesight checked!'

The smile he gave at this remark was the most genuine Jaz had ever seen him give, revealing even white teeth, grey eyes gleaming warmly, taking years off him as he looked almost boyish.

Wow! Jaz allowed inwardly, finding herself the mesmerized one now.

Which wasn't going to do her, or anyone else, any good whatsoever!

Beau gave a rueful shake of his head. 'Are you suggesting that I've become short-sighted in my old age?' he drawled ruefully.

Old age! When he smiled like that he definitely only looked in his late thirties, and rakishly attractive to boot. Too much so for her peace of mind!

She quickly drank down her cooling coffee before standing up noisily, not quite meeting his gaze now. 'Time I got back to work,' she mumbled awkwardly.

'Jaz...?' he murmured softly as she hurried across the room to the door.

She paused, drawing in a controlling breath, drawing

back her shoulders before turning to face him. 'Yes?' she prompted tautly.

He walked softly across the room to stand in front of her, his gaze questioning now. 'I'm sure I can't be the first man to tell you how beautiful you are—'

'Now you're going too far!' She frowned in rebuke, disappointment her main emotion.

She had actually been starting to like him, appreciated rather than resented his old-fashioned view that shifting rocks was 'a man's work'. But now he was just being deliberately cruel.

'Thanks for the coffee, Mr Garrett, but the entertainment's over; I'm going back to work,' she told him abruptly before turning away.

Strong fingers dug into her upper arms as he reached out to hold her firmly in front of him, his gaze searching as she glared up at him resentfully.

Living in the village had been far from easy since her mother had run off, village people, as Jaz knew to her cost, having long memories. But she had been born here, had no intention of being driven out of her birthright because of the viciousness of some of the gossip. And, with time, it had lessened, finally fading almost completely; she certainly didn't need Beau Garrett, a complete stranger to the area, coming here and tormenting her in another way!

His frown had turned to puzzlement now. 'Jaz—' He broke off as a knock sounded on the back door.

'Hello? Anyone home?' Without waiting for an answer to his call, Dennis, the builder, opened the door to look expectantly into the room.

Where, Jaz knew, she and the famous Beau Garrett were standing far too close for two people who were supposed to be relative strangers!

CHAPTER FIVE

BILLS, bills, nothing but— What…?

Jaz's hand shook as she held the single sheet of paper, staring disbelievingly at the single sentence printed there. Only four words, but, nevertheless, those four words had the impact on her that they were obviously supposed to.

'Like mother, like daughter'.

Like mother, like daughter—except Jaz was nothing like her mother. Nothing!

She flung the letter down onto the cluttered desk-top in the garden-centre office where she had been opening her post, before standing up to pace restlessly, her gaze returning again and again to that unsigned letter.

What did it mean? In what way was she supposed to be like her mother?

The envelope, she suddenly realized. It would have a stamp on it with the time and place of postage, plus the address would have to have been written there too.

No, the address had been printed by computer too— so much for her amateur sleuthing! And there was no postage stamp on it. Which meant it must have been delivered by hand.

Jaz recoiled from the thought that it might have been someone local who had sent the anonymous letter to her, her stomach churning with distaste that she might actually know someone capable of doing this.

But what other explanation was there? The letter had been laying on the floor with all the other letters delivered while she'd been out at work all day, gathered up in their number and opened in all innocence of its contents.

'Anyone here?'

Jaz easily recognized that voice, moving quickly to gather up the letter and its envelope, to push them into the top drawer of the desk just as Beau Garrett let himself into the office.

'Yes?' she prompted slightly breathlessly, standing protectively in front of the desk—as if she thought that damning letter were going to leap out of its own volition and present itself to this man!

Maybe she should show it to him? Maybe if she could share it with someone it wouldn't seem quite so—

Ridiculous, she instantly told herself irritably. It was unpleasant—unbelievably so, if she were honest with herself!—but not anything that concerned this man. Certainly nothing she could 'share' with him, or anyone else.

Beau frowned across the room at her. 'Are you okay?'

She swallowed hard, forcing herself to relax as she smiled at him reassuringly. 'Of course.'

His frown didn't alter. 'You're looking a little pale…?'

Jaz gave a dismissive grimace. 'I'm probably hungry. Besides,' she added ruefully, 'I've just received the electricity bill!'

Beau gave a derisive smile. 'That would do it.' He nodded understandingly. 'And talking of hungry—I'm just on my way out to the pub for dinner. I saw your light on, and wondered if, like me, you felt like giving cooking a miss for this evening?'

Jaz stared at him. Had Beau Garrett just invited her

out to dinner? Albeit the pub at the other end of the village...

Yes, he had. And she could easily guess the reason for it!

They hadn't parted on too friendly terms earlier today, Jaz making good her escape from the kitchen with Dennis's timely arrival. And she had left promptly at five o'clock without speaking to Beau Garrett again.

The man obviously felt guilty about his teasing earlier today!

He raised mocking dark brows at her lack of response. 'Pub. Food,' he enunciated slowly. 'My treat,' he added as she continued to look at him without speaking.

That last remark evoked a response, her cheeks colouring angrily. 'I'm not in need of anyone's charity, Mr Garrett,' she snapped waspishly. *Least of all yours,* her tone clearly implied.

His expression darkened irritably. 'And I'm not in the business of offering anyone charity—Miss Logan,' he bit out harshly. 'Merely suggesting we eat dinner together, and as such ensuring that you have enough strength to shift another load of junk from my garden tomorrow!'

She deserved his impatient anger, and she knew it; she was just feeling shaken, and not a little sensitive, from receiving that anonymous letter.

But what was it, after all? Amateur hour, that's what it was. Probably just some kid who liked playing with his computer and had read too many Agatha Christies than was good for him!

'Besides,' Beau Garrett added abruptly, 'I hate eating alone.'

When he put it like that...!

Jaz gave a heavy sigh, relaxing slightly. 'Sorry if I sounded ungrateful,' she grimaced. 'Dinner at the pub sounds wonderful,' she accepted gracefully.

It would also give her time and distance from that horrible letter. And when she got back later this evening she would throw the thing straight in the bin.

'Do you have time to wait while I change out of these old clothes?' She had actually changed out of her working clothes when she'd got in half an hour ago, but these faded denims and one of her father's old jumpers, although clean, were almost as disreputable.

Beau gave a decisive shake of his head. 'You look fine. And I've been assured that they do ''a marvelous steak'' at the pub,' he added more practically.

Jaz moved to pick up her heavy coat, laughing softly at his perfect imitation of Barbara Scott at the village shop. 'Did you ever think of taking up acting?' she prompted interestedly after locking up and following him out to the Range Rover.

'Never!' he assured with a barely suppressed shudder. 'Did you never think of doing something other than follow in your father's footsteps?'

Jaz gave him a considering look, that look cut short as the interior light of the powerful vehicle clicked off overhead. 'Saved by the light,' she drawled. 'And, no, I never considered doing anything else. I love gardening, love collecting the seeds, nurturing the seedlings, seeing them grow into beautiful blooms. My grandmother—the designer of the rock garden,' she reminded dryly, 'she loved it too. You might say it's in the blood,' she added teasingly. And then felt the chill of ice in her veins.

As that anonymous letter had already stated, she was her mother's daughter too!

No, she wasn't, Jaz decided just as firmly. Her mother had been flighty and irresponsible, but most of all self-centred; none of which Jaz believed herself to be.

'But you didn't properly answer my question,' she prompted Beau pointedly.

He gave her a brief grin. 'No, I didn't, did I?'

And he wasn't going to do so, either, his tone clearly implied.

Oh, well, if he didn't want to talk about himself, that was his choice, Jaz shrugged inwardly. Although he was singularly different from any other man she knew if that really were the case; on the few dates she had accepted over the years those men couldn't seem to talk about anything else but themselves!

Date? Having a meal at the local pub with Beau Garrett couldn't be considered a date. She—

'What are you thinking about now?' Beau gave her a sideways glance as he drove the short distance to the pub.

'Nothing,' she dismissed, warm colour in her cheeks; there was no way she could tell this man what she had been thinking.

She still had no idea whether Beau Garrett was married or not. But she did know that, even if he wasn't, she certainly wasn't the type of woman to attract him. He was much older, not just because he was aged in his late thirties or early forties, but because he had far more experience of life than her. His arrogantly aristocratic good looks put him well out of her league. And for years he had been at the centre of the world of television, surrounded by beautiful and sophisticated women. Jaz well knew that, despite his earlier teasing words, she had neither of those attributes.

'You aren't having dinner with a married man, if that's what's bothering you,' Beau drawled derisively.

'How did you do that?' she gasped.

'It really wasn't that difficult, Jaz,' he assured her mockingly. 'You asked me the other day whether my "family" would be joining me.' He gave a dismissive shrug, turning the Range Rover into the pub car park before turning off the engine to turn in his seat, his expression grim. 'I was married once, but that was over years ago,' he bit out harshly. 'I haven't been a monk since, but there's no one currently in my life.'

'You really don't need to tell me any of this.' Jaz couldn't quite meet his gaze, her cheeks coloured hotly now.

'No, I don't,' he acknowledged abruptly, opening the door and getting out of the vehicle. 'But I thought you might like to know anyway,' he added scornfully. 'Bearing in mind your warnings that this is a small village and people like to talk.'

Jaz followed slowly. She had wanted to know his marital status, certainly didn't want to have dinner with a married man, even as innocently as this was; there had been enough talk about her family over the years without her adding to the gossip. But it somehow felt uncomfortable to know that a man as sophisticated as Beau had been all too aware of her misgivings.

She could comfort herself by claiming she was out of practise in these things, but as she had never been in practise in the first place…!

'I must seem extremely unsophisticated to you,' she muttered as the two of them walked towards the warmth of the pub.

'Refreshingly naïve,' Beau corrected lightly, reaching forward to open the door for her.

For naïve read gauche and silly, Jaz accepted heavily as she stepped into the tastefully lit and furnished pub, a glowing warmth giving off by the log fire at one end of the room.

Beau looked around him interestedly. 'I didn't know places like this really existed,' he murmured appreciatively.

'Ye Olde Country Pub.' Jaz nodded smilingly. 'I'm told that the beer's quite good too,' she added derisively.

'Hey, give me a break; I've lived in London for the last thirty-nine years!' Beau chided as they made their way through the crowded room to a table closer to the fire.

Was it only Jaz's imagination or was there a slight drop in conversation as they made their way across the room? And if there was, was it because of Beau Garrett's presence here, or her own?

'Good evening, Jaz,' Tom, the jovial landlord greeted warmly. 'We don't see you in here too often,' he added welcomingly.

Mainly because she couldn't afford to come in here too often. Although she didn't think it would go down too well with the locals anyway if she, a lone female, were to spend much time in here!

But it was as if Tom's warm welcome had triggered a switch, several other people greeting her as Beau ordered their drinks. Confirming for Jaz that there definitely had been a lull in the conversation when they'd come in, whether deliberate or accidental.

Or maybe she was just becoming over-sensitive because of that stupid anonymous letter? It certainly hadn't helped her self-confidence any!

'They seem quite a friendly lot,' Beau remarked as

they took their drinks, and a bar menu, across to the table with them.

Jaz recognized most of the people in the room, knew for the main part that they were friendly. Except it could have been one of them that had sent her that letter...

No, she was being silly now; better to continue thinking it had been some teenager who had nothing better to do. She certainly couldn't go around suspecting everyone she met.

'They are,' she confirmed briskly before turning determinedly to look at the menu.

Everything there made her mouth water, from the home-made chicken and ham pie, to the highly recommended sirloin steak with fries, mushrooms and onion rings. She couldn't remember the last time she had eaten a steak!

'Vegetable pasta, please.' She selected the cheapest thing on the menu before closing it firmly.

'Really?' Beau raised dark brows. 'I quite fancied the sirloin myself.'

Jaz swallowed as her mouth began to water again. She liked pasta, wouldn't have ordered it if she didn't, but it would be sheer torture to sit here and eat it next to Beau while he tucked into a juicy steak with all the trimmings!

'You aren't a vegetarian, are you?' he prompted interestedly.

She had considered it a few years ago—she had a feeling that most teenagers did at some time, but she had only to smell bacon frying in a pan to know that she could never be a true vegetarian. And her reaction to Beau's mention of steak only confirmed that!

'No,' she confirmed ruefully. 'But it's very nice of you to invite me out, Beau, and I wouldn't want to—'

'Two sirloin steaks,' Beau told the barmaid, Tom's daughter, as she came over to take their order, Tom's wife Bella cooking in the kitchen. 'Medium?' he prompted Jaz as Sharon waited to see how they would like their meat cooked.

'Lovely. Thank you,' Jaz added awkwardly. 'How are the wedding arrangements coming along, Sharon?' she prompted the other girl to cover some of her embarrassment at having Beau order her food in this arrogant way.

'Fine,' Sharon confirmed abruptly, a tall leggy blonde who made no effort to hide the fact that she couldn't wait to retire from being a barmaid in her father's pub after her wedding in three weeks time to a local farmer. 'It will be about fifteen minutes.' Her voice warmed considerably when she spoke to Beau.

Jaz didn't listen to Beau's answer, pretending a sudden interest in one of the prints on the wall beside her, while inside she acknowledged with a heavy heart that some people's opinion of her would never change. Her mother had run off with someone else's husband, and so Jaz was viewed with the same suspicion when it came to any other woman's boyfriend or husband. It was ridiculous, of course, but fact nonetheless.

She turned back to Beau just in time to see the look of admiration on his face as he watched Sharon walk away, her black skirt a little tighter than necessary, her legs long and shapely beneath its short length.

And why shouldn't he look at the other woman admiringly; in comparison with his own companion, in her baggy jumper and patched denims, Sharon looked positively elegant!

Jaz was smiling derisively by the time Beau became aware of her gaze, dark brows rising questioningly over mocking grey eyes as he returned her gaze speculatively.

'It's a man thing.' He shrugged unapologetically.

'Sharon is very pretty,' Jaz nodded noncommittally.

'With legs like those she could look like Godzilla and get away with it!' Beau grinned, that scar down the side of his face once again giving him a piratical look.

Her own legs weren't bad, Jaz thought disgruntledly. Except that she was rarely out of jeans or trousers in order to show them off! Maybe next time—

Next time? She caught herself up short. What did she mean, next time? She didn't seriously think that Beau was going to make taking her out to dinner a regular occurrence, did she? Fat chance!

'Why did you say you wanted pasta when it was really the steak you wanted?'

It took a couple of seconds for Jaz to realize that Beau had completely caught her off-guard by this sudden change of subject. But how could she explain, without sounding totally pathetic, that she always chose the cheapest thing off the menu on the rare occasions she was invited to eat out?

She moistened dry lips. 'I wouldn't like to take advantage of your generosity by—'

'Jaz, who's responsible for giving you such a lack of self-worth that you don't even order the food you really want from a pub menu? Whoever it is, you really don't need them in your life,' he added grimly. '"With friends like that you don't need enemies",' he quoted disgustedly.

It wasn't any one person who had given her that sense of making herself as inconspicuous as possible, more a series of circumstances. But they weren't circumstances she intended sharing with Beau Garrett!

'I think you're reading far too much into this, Beau,' she answered derisively. 'I was merely brought up to believe that it isn't polite to take advantage of another person's generosity.'

'Let's get one thing clear, Jaz.' Beau turned in his seat so that he was looking directly at her, his expression no less grim. 'I am not being generous, in fact you're the one doing me a favour; as I've already told you, I hate to eat out alone!'

No doubt, being who he was, his face easily recognizable—as was obvious by the surreptitious looks he had already received from the other patrons here—eating out alone could be something of a problem for him, encouraging people to actually come up and start talking to him. Something she was sure, even on such short acquaintance, that Beau would not enjoy.

'In that case,' she relaxed slightly '...I may have dessert too!'

'Good for you.' He nodded approvingly. 'Who knows, then you might even be able to help me uproot some of those overgrown fruit bushes tomorrow!'

Of course, she had completely forgotten she was doing a job of work for this man. She would do well in future to remember that was his only interest in her.

CHAPTER SIX

NOT that there was too much chance of Jaz doing that over the next half-hour or so as Sharon seemed to go out of her way to make sure Beau would definitely know her the next time they met, curvaceous hips swaying above those long legs when she delivered the food to their table fifteen minutes later, her smile friendly towards him as she went through the list of condiments he could have with his steak, her voice huskily inviting when she returned ten minutes later to see if everything was okay with their meal.

If Jaz had been asked, she could have said the only thing wrong with her meal was these constant interruptions from a woman who should know better when she was about to be married in three weeks time!

'Everything is fine, thanks,' Beau responded lightly to the enquiry, the smile still curving his lips when he turned and found Jaz frowning at him. He gave a rueful shrug. 'She's just being friendly.'

Friendly, my foot. What Sharon was being was deliberately irritating to Jaz. She had gone to school with the other woman, the two of them of similar age, Sharon amongst the nastiest of taunters when Jaz's mother had run off with another man. Jaz had no idea what made people so cruel, but she very much doubted that Sharon had changed that much from when they had both been seventeen.

'Hey?' Beau was looking at her questioningly now. 'This sort of thing happens all the time,' he dismissed disinterestedly. 'It's the show. People know my face and, as such, think they know me.'

Jaz wondered if he really didn't think that his devastating good looks could have had anything to do with Sharon's flirtatious behaviour towards him.

She gave herself a mental shake, knowing she was reacting badly to the over-friendly manner of a silly woman she knew would take great delight in knowing she had scored a direct hit with her behaviour. Besides, Jaz chided herself impatiently, she wasn't out on a date with Beau Garrett, merely sharing a meal with him because he hated to eat alone.

She gave a nod. 'I think you underestimate your own attraction there, Beau,' she derided. 'But you're right about Sharon being friendly, in fact she's being deliberately provocative because the two of us have never got on.'

'Hey,' he chided, turning in his seat to lightly curve her jaw and raise her face to his. 'I didn't say it was all due to the show,' he drawled mockingly.

Jaz laughed, as she knew she was supposed to. Beau may like to give the impression that he was cold and arrogant, but somehow Jaz thought that wasn't the whole story. He was self-confident, yes, self-sufficient too, and his often ruthless interviewing of the guests on his talk show proved that he really didn't suffer fools gladly either, but underneath that aloof exterior Jaz already knew he was a much warmer, caring person than he would like people to believe.

And she was rapidly becoming light-headed from the unaccustomed glass of red wine, the warmth from the fire, the good food, and the company of this attractive, sophisticated man.

The touch of his hand against her jaw wasn't helping, either, his skin warm and firm against hers.

'I should have asked earlier.' He spoke huskily, his gaze guarded now as it searched her flushed face. 'Is there anyone who is likely to object to your coming out to dinner with me like this?' He frowned darkly.

'Anyone—? Oh.' Jaz could feel the warmth deepen in her cheeks as his meaning became clear. 'No,' she said abruptly. 'There's no one like that.'

His gaze darkened intently. 'Has there ever been?'

'No...' She swallowed hard, wondering exactly where this conversation was leading. If anywhere!

He gave a disgusted shake of his head. 'Confirming my impression that there's a distinct lack of red-blooded men in Aberton!'

Jaz spluttered with laughter at the unexpected remark. 'What makes you say that?'

He grimaced. 'There was a definite difference in ratio of men to women at Madelaine's drinks party last week. I also had the feeling I was being assessed as regards suitable marriageable material. On several levels!' he added derisively. 'Not least of all by my hostess!'

No doubt he had been, although Jaz, thankfully, had already left before that had started. She would hate to think that Beau thought of her as one of that number.

'Poor Madelaine,' she murmured ruefully. 'She's very nice, don't you think?' Madelaine was one of the few people who had been kind to her after her mother ran off so abruptly. Far from what Jaz might have expected, the older woman had in fact been one of the few people to be kind to her.

'Oh, very nice,' he mimicked mockingly, his hand at last falling away from her chin as he lifted his glass and took a drink of his beer. 'You were right about this, by the way; it is good,' he assured appreciatively.

End of that particular conversation, Jaz easily guessed, this man shying away from any suggestion that he might be looking for anything more than a home in Aberton.

A warning to her as well as women like Sharon and Madelaine…? Probably not, she decided ruefully. She doubted he would have invited her to share a meal with him if he found her the teeniest little bit of a threat to his bachelor status.

Well, that was a really confidence-boosting realization. She—

'Hello, you two,' an over-jovial voice greeted intrusively.

Dennis Davis of all people, Jaz realized with a certain amount of dismay, her smile forced as she looked up at him.

Her father's contemporary, as well as being an unreliable builder, Dennis's job also allowed him to be one of the busiest gossips in the village. The chances of her shared meal with the new celebrity in the village escaping notice had already been slim, but with Dennis's appearance in the pub it was now non-existent! Jaz could guarantee that by five o'clock tomorrow evening every inhabitant of the village would know that John Logan's daughter had spent the evening with the famous Beau Garrett. Worse, that Janie Logan's daughter had been seen out with him!

'Davis.' Beau nodded aloofly to the other man.

Dennis grinned unabashedly. 'I've just called in for a pint on my way home from work.'

Beau's brows rose over mocking grey eyes. 'I thought you packed in for the day two hours ago?'

'On your roof, yes,' Dennis confirmed brightly, still wearing the paint-daubed overalls he had been working in earlier. 'Can't work on a roof once it's dark, but there are plenty of other inside jobs I can be getting on with.'

As far as Jaz was aware, the only 'inside job' Dennis got on with at five o'clock was to visit a certain married lady in a village five miles away. Dennis lived in a cottage with his spinster sister, Margaret, and the arrangement suited him as well as his sister. But that didn't mean he couldn't have a 'friend', especially a married one who wasn't in a position to make any demands on him.

Dennis was what the village called a *character*, excusing his less-than-reputable behaviour on those grounds. Jaz, in view of how her mother had behaved, had a totally different name for him!

'I see,' Beau returned dryly, seeming to already know the older man well enough to realize it wasn't work that had delayed Dennis's arrival home. 'Well, don't let us keep you from your ''pint'',' he added pointedly as the other man seemed inclined to linger.

Dennis nodded reluctantly. 'I'll leave you two alone, then.' He shot Jaz a totally speculative look before leaving.

'Oh, dear,' Jaz grimaced once the other man had left. 'Our innocent meal out together will have become something totally different by the time Dennis gets through talking about it,' she explained at Beau's questioning look.

'Let it,' he rasped scathingly. 'Maybe it will help to keep other women off my back!'

In other words, she could be used as a shield for this man against any relationship-minded women in the area!

Not exactly flattering. Considering her naïvety, and Beau's obvious air of sophistication, not exactly believable, either. And certainly no good for her reputation.

'I don't think it was your ''back'' they were interested in,' she came back waspishly.

His expression became grim, his eyes cold as he raised a hand to the livid scar down the right side of his face. 'The front isn't exactly pretty,' he rasped harshly.

They all had their sensitive points, it seemed...

Jaz gave him a calm, considering look. 'I'm sure you could have plastic surgery to lessen the scar, if it bothers you that much.'

His gaze became glacial now. 'It doesn't ''bother'' me,' he bit out coldly, stiffly aloof now.

'But your television programme—'

'I said it doesn't bother me,' he rasped.

'But—'

'If you've finished your meal we may as well leave,' he cut in icily, pushing his own plate away as he prepared to go.

It may not bother him, but it was obviously a sore point, one that Jaz, in view of their abrupt departure, was now sorry she had pursued.

'I've finished,' she confirmed evenly. 'And I'll be quite happy to walk back if you—'

'Don't be ridiculous,' he cut in scathingly, standing up abruptly. 'I brought you here, I'll take you home.'

'This isn't London, Beau—'

'I'm well aware of that!' he snapped enigmatically.

'I'll be quite safe walking home—'

'It isn't a question of safety,' Beau rasped. 'Although it's certainly a factor.'

Jaz wrapped her scarf about her neck before following him outside into the cold night air. 'What is it a question of, then?' she teased, hoping to lighten his mood somewhat.

They had been getting along just fine until the subject of his scar had been introduced to the conversation. Her own fault for pursuing it, she accepted, but the truth was she had enjoyed herself this evening more than she had for a long time. It would be a pity for them to part on bad terms now.

He glanced back at her in the semi-darkness of the car park. 'You really want to know?'

Her stomach gave an uncomfortable lurch at his reluctance to answer her; he didn't appear to be a man who suffered from that emotion too often. 'I really want to know,' she told him firmly.

Beau stopped to turn to her. 'Okay, then. The truth is, you look too tired to make it the half a mile back to your home!'

Well, that was certainly honest, Jaz accepted ruefully. Not exactly flattering, but honest.

She gave a self-derisive smile. 'I really am much stronger than I look, you know.'

'I hope so, for your sake,' he returned grimly. 'Otherwise you may not make it to the end of the week!'

Not only did he sound as if he didn't have a lot of faith in her landscape gardening abilities, his remark was also extremely patronizing. She had never not completed a job, and he had already heard the praises of her satisfied customers to prove it.

Jaz eyed him frowningly. 'Is that why you invited me out to dinner?'

'What do you think?' He eyed her coldly now.

Jaz opened her mouth to make a cutting reply, stopping as a car swung into the car park, its headlights briefly illuminating the two of them as they faced each other like antagonists.

Because that's exactly how Jaz felt at this moment. She wasn't some charity case he needed to bestow his largesse upon. In fact, she had offered to pay for her own meal earlier and been very firmly verbally slapped down.

It had seemed petty at the time to argue the point with him, as it was just as impossible now with other people getting out of their parked vehicle, but that didn't mean he had heard the last on the subject!

'Jaz! How lovely to see you,' greeted a voice that Jaz instantly recognized as being Madelaine Wilder's.

She turned to see the other woman just getting out of her Jaguar saloon, the figure emerging from the passenger side of the vehicle identifying itself as the major.

'And Beau too,' the other woman realized delightedly, a fragile blonde with beautiful china-doll features that belied her forty-five years, looking very attractive in a silky suit of pale mauve. 'How wonderful—we can all have dinner together!' Blue eyes glowed with pleasure as she strolled over to join them.

'I'm afraid not,' Beau was the one to answer evenly, stepping forward to take a proprietal hold of Jaz's arm. 'Jaz and I have already eaten,' he added with what, to Jaz at least, definitely sounded like relief.

'Oh, what a pity…' Madelaine's smoothly perfect features echoed the disappointment in her voice. 'But perhaps you could join us for a drink before you go?' she invited hopefully.

'Yes, do join us for a drink, old boy. You too, Jaz,' the major added somewhat belatedly.

Quite what he was a major of, no one, not even the biggest gossips, had actually been able to ascertain in the twenty years he had lived in the village, although he occasionally dropped remarks into the conversation about his 'time in India'…

Jaz looked at the other couple, both the major and Madelaine very smartly dressed, the major in blazer and grey trousers, a regimental tie knotted precisely at his throat, and from experience, Madelaine's silk suit would have a designer label. Even Beau was looking expensively casual, but Jaz, in her disreputable jumper and patched jeans, was definitely out of their league.

'I'm really sorry—' once again Beau was the one to answer for the both of them '—but I have some work to do.'

'Really?' Madelaine's beautiful face lit up with interest. 'What are you—?'

'I'm afraid we really do have to go,' Beau cut in firmly, his fingers tightening pointedly on Jaz's arm.

'Yes,' she put in brightly. 'I—have some things to do myself.' She wasn't lying, either, she always had 'some things to do'. 'Maybe next time,' she added warmly to take some of the sting out of Beau's abruptness.

'Of course,' the major accepted smoothly.

Aged in his mid-sixties, twenty years older than Madelaine, he had obviously been waging some sort of romantic campaign in her direction the last couple of years. To no avail as far as Madelaine was concerned. With the possible exception of when Madelaine needed a male escort to some social function or other.

Not that Jaz could exactly blame the other woman for feeling that way. Madelaine was a very attractive and wealthy widow of only forty-five, whereas the major, although pleasant enough, was definitely something of an old duffer. But 'harmless enough', as Madelaine had once girlishly confided in Jaz.

Although he was obviously pleased that she and Beau—especially Beau, Jaz suspected!—weren't about to intrude on his evening out with Madelaine.

'Lovely to have seen you again, Beau,' Madelaine stood on tiptoe to kiss him lightly on his left cheek. 'Jaz,' she added affectionately before repeating the gesture, at once enveloping Jaz in the waft of her expensive perfume.

'Whew!' Beau muttered thankfully once the two of them were at last seated in his Range Rover. 'I don't know what it is about that woman—she's certainly pleasant enough—but I just want to take to the hills every time I see her!'

Jaz's eyes widened at the admission as she stared at him in the semi-darkness, knowing by the look of confused self-disgust on his face that he meant what he said. Even if he didn't understand the feeling.

She chuckled softly. 'Coward!' She shook her head disbelievingly.

'Without doubt,' he confirmed unabashedly, turning the key in the ignition. 'I came here to get away from well-meaning, predatory females, not meet more of them!' he added grimly before turning his concentration towards his driving.

Leaving Jaz to wonder what he thought *she* was. Obviously not predatory. But did Beau not see her as female, either?

Doubtful, she acknowledged self-derisively. Or, if he did, it was something in the way of a little sister, someone who needed looking after. In any case, it was obvious Beau didn't see her as any sort of threat to his solitary existence.

She hadn't thought she was, either. But not for the reason Beau obviously did. She simply wasn't interested in the complications of loving someone enough to give over her future happiness into their hands. A cliché perhaps, a direct result of her parents'broken marriage, but it was nonetheless the way she felt about love and marriage.

Then why did she feel this sense of disappointment that Beau didn't even see her as female, let alone attractive…?

'What did I say or do now?' Beau sighed wearily, obviously aware of her preoccupation, if not the reason for it.

'Absolutely nothing,' she assured him crisply, annoyed with herself for even thinking such things. 'So you are here to work, after all?' she prompted interestedly.

'No, I'm not,' he answered flatly. 'I only said that to get away from "the Odd Couple".'

Jaz gave a reproving frown at his description of Madelaine and the major. 'You can be extremely cutting when you want, can't you?' she told Beau as he gave her a questioning glance. 'Madelaine is one of the nicest people I know, and the major is—well, he's harmless enough, to quote Madelaine! And they aren't a couple,' she added defensively, knowing Madelaine wouldn't like this highly eligible man to think that they were.

Beau's mouth twisted derisively. 'She just feels sorry for him every now and then and throws him a few crumbs of human kindness, is that it?' he rasped harshly.

Jaz gasped. 'I take back what I said just now,' she told him breathlessly as he parked the Range Rover outside the garden centre. 'You aren't just cutting—you're deliberately nasty!' She glared at him accusingly.

After all, what did he really know about any of them? The major. Madelaine. Even her. Nothing really, and yet he had already sat in judgement of them all—and found them wanting!

Beau turned in his seat to look at her, his arm resting on the steering wheel, a mocking smile now curving his lips. 'That's been said before,' he drawled unconcernedly. '"Sticks and stones", Jaz.' He shrugged dismissively.

'Not at all,' she told him emotionally. 'And if it's been said before, don't you think it might actually have some merit?'

He gave a dismissive grimace. 'I've never tried to win any popularity contests.'

That was obvious from the guests he chose for his television programme, and the way he interviewed them, both guaranteed to be controversial. 'Compulsive viewing', Jaz vaguely remembered one reviewer enthusing approvingly. Maybe so, but it was ultimately Beau Garrett they were referring to and not his guests.

'What's the matter, Jaz?' Beau cut tauntingly into her thoughts. 'Decided I'm really not a nice person, after all?'

'I'm not sure that I have ever said I thought otherwise!' she was stung into replying.

He shrugged unconcernedly, eyes glittering in the darkness. 'Then one more insult isn't going to matter, is it?' he dismissed derisively, and before Jaz could even begin to guess what he meant by that remark he had reached out to clasp her upper arms and pull her towards him, his mouth claiming hers with punishing determination.

At which point Jaz knew that the last thing she felt was insulted! Dazed. Surprised. Mesmerized, even. But she was too stunned by the unexpectedness of the kiss to feel insulted.

Following that initial surprise she found herself filled with a glowing warmth, trembling from head to foot, her whole body liquifying as she leaned into him weakly, lips burning as Beau kissed her with a thoroughness that was completely beyond her experience, his arms firmly holding her body curved against the hardness of his.

'Oh!' she gasped some time later—how much time?—as he finally raised his head and thrust her away from him.

'I told you that you have a very kissable mouth,' Beau rasped unapologetically, his expression grim, hands once again gripping the steering-wheel. 'Now get out of here—before I do something to really shock you!'

Jaz 'got', scrambling inelegantly down from the Range Rover to hurry over to the small cottage where she lived in the grounds of the garden centre, not looking back as she heard the roar of the vehicle's engine as Beau took off at great speed.

What had triggered that? she wondered dazedly as she leant back against her closed front door. Her 'kissable mouth', Beau had claimed, but surely it had to be more than that?

Like what? Beau actually being attracted to her? Somehow, despite his earlier kindness, she didn't think that was the answer. Then what was?

She didn't know, really didn't have the experience to try to fathom a man like Beau Garrett. In which case, the best thing, surely, was for her to keep well away from him?

Easier said than done, when she was actually working on his garden for the foreseeable future!

Although, after this disastrous end to the evening, she didn't think he would be too happy to spend too much time in her company, either...

It was only later—much later, her jobs all done for the evening—as she lay in bed trying desperately to sleep, that she remembered the anonymous letter she had received earlier today. Remembered also that it was still in the top drawer of her desk, that with Beau's arrival earlier she had totally forgotten to destroy it!

CHAPTER SEVEN

'So would you like to tell me what the hell is going on?'

Jaz stared at Beau around the half open door to the cottage as he stood angrily on her front doorstep, clutching her robe to her as she did so, her hair caught up in a towel to prevent the steam from her bath-water frizzing it into even wilder disarray.

How did he know?

What did he know?

As far as she was aware she had destroyed that letter first thing this morning, before anyone else had an opportunity to see it. And yet here Beau now was, standing on her doorstep at nine o'clock at night, demanding to know 'what was going on?'!

Although she had worked on his garden most of the day this was the first time she had seen him since his abrupt departure the evening before, the memory of the reason for that abruptness bringing the colour into her cheeks.

She blinked, shaking her head. 'I don't know what—' She broke off as Beau walked past her into the cottage. 'Come in, why don't you?' she muttered disgruntledly as she closed the door behind him, turning to find him frowning down at her in the dimly lit hallway, instantly finding the cottage even smaller than usual when dominated by this man's forceful presence.

'Have I caught you in the middle of something?' Dark brows were raised as he looked at her standing

there in her bathrobe. It was all too obviously the only
clothing she was wearing, her legs and feet bare, as was
her throat above the vee of the robe.

Her cheeks felt even hotter. 'I was taking a bath when
you knocked on the door.' Battered on it would have
been a more fitting description of the thunderous noise
he had made on the cottage door—she had thought there
had to be a fire, at least! But apart from Beau's angry
opening remark, he didn't look as if he were in the
midst of an emergency.

'Oh.' He looked slightly perplexed now.

'Yes,' Jaz acknowledged dryly. 'If you would like to
wait in the sitting room…' She opened the door to the
left of them, glad she had lit a fire in there earlier. The
shabby room looked much more comfortable when
warmed by a coal fire. 'I'll—I'll just go and put some
clothes on.' She really would have to try and learn a
little social coolness, she inwardly remonstrated with
herself; this constant blushing was extremely juvenile!

Beau's mouth curved into a mocking smile, his gaze
speculative. 'Don't bother on my account,' he murmured huskily.

Jaz gave him a glaring look. 'I'm "bothering" on
my own account, thank you.'

He shrugged. 'Okay, go ahead. As you suggested, I'll
be waiting in here.' He strolled into the sitting room.

Jaz didn't wait any longer, hurrying up the stairs as
fast as her bare legs would carry her, quickly taking out
clean underwear and a jumper and jeans, removing the
towel from her hair before pulling them on hastily, feeling much more self-contained once she had some
clothes on. Being in Beau's company was intimidating
enough at any time, standing in front of him half

dressed, while he was fully clothed, was something guaranteed to lessen her own self-confidence.

And after the way they had parted the evening before she needed all of that she could find!

She had no idea what had induced Beau to kiss her in the way that he had, had lain awake for hours as the incident played over and over again in her mind, feeling tired and disgruntled this morning when she'd climbed out of bed at her usual seven o'clock, the thought of shortly seeing Beau again not helping her mood any.

Not that she need have worried about that at all; Beau's Range Rover had been missing all day, as had the man himself, neither having returned when she'd left at four o'clock.

But he had returned now—and he was obviously upset about something!

But he couldn't know about that anonymous letter she had received; now that she had destroyed it, only she and the person who had written it could possibly know about that. So what was bothering him?

Only one way to find out…

Beau was staring into the glowing fire when she quietly entered the sitting room a few minutes later, giving her a moment's respite before he turned and saw her.

Something seemed to catch in her throat every time she looked at this man, her breathing suddenly constricted, her pulse racing as she knew herself to be completely aware of him.

He looked slightly incongruous standing amidst the scruffy comfort of her tiny sitting room, only space for a sagging sofa and matching chair, the table beside the chair piled high with gardening magazines and catalogues.

As if sensing her presence, he glanced up, the glow

from the fire throwing his face into stark relief, emphasizing that scar that ran from his eye to his jaw. 'Mesmerizing,' he murmured ruefully.

Although she knew her appearance to be vastly improved by the clothes and freshly brushed hair, somehow Jaz didn't think he was referring to her!

Beau moved abruptly, so that he now had his back towards the fire. 'Feel better?' He raised mocking brows.

'Yes, thank you,' she answered primly, hoping he would now put that glow in her cheeks down to the warmth from the fire—although somehow she doubted it; this man knew exactly what effect he had on her!

How could he be in any doubts after her response to him the night before?

She straightened, her gaze now meeting his unflinchingly. 'What can I do for you?'

He gave a derisive smile. 'I think it might be better if I didn't answer that!'

She gave an impatient sigh at his deliberate mockery, knowing that the kiss of last night couldn't possibly mean to him what it had meant to her. He was an experienced man of the world, couldn't have failed to be aware of her inexperience, even when it came to kissing a man. 'Beau—'

'Okay.' He held up a silencing hand. 'You can start by telling me why I had to suffer innuendos and rib nudging remarks from Dennis Davis when I arrived home this evening. Why Mrs Scott, when I called in at the village shop to get something for my dinner, remarked how very...*kind* it was of me to take such an interest in *poor* Jaz,' he continued grimly, eyes narrowed. 'And why, when Madelaine Wilder "popped over" a short time ago to say how sorry she was we couldn't all have dinner together last night—' his mouth twisted scathingly '—she was at great pains to tell me how deserving you were of meeting ''a nice young man''. I doubt she was referring to me by that last remark, by the way!' he concluded self-derisively.

Jaz had felt the colour slowly fading from her cheeks as Beau had related each incident that had brought him to her doorstep this evening. She wasn't sure she wouldn't almost have preferred him to have been referring to that anonymous letter, after all! Almost...

Dennis, despite his outer pleasantness, she had never liked, Barbara Scott was well-meaning, she was sure, and Madelaine only had her best interests at heart. All of which didn't mean that Jaz didn't wish they would all just mind their own business!

She moistened dry lips. 'Can I offer you a cup of tea or coffee?' she delayed, her mind racing as to exactly how she could answer him. 'I'm afraid I don't have anything stronger in the house; my father wasn't a drinker, and, apart from the odd social glass of wine, neither am I.'

'Jaz—'

'I fancy a coffee myself,' she continued brightly, turning to leave the room. 'If you have time, of course?' she paused to add.

Beau shrugged, his narrowed gaze not leaving her face for a moment. 'I have nothing else to do this evening,' he began slowly.

'How flattering!' Jaz came back with deliberate facetiousness.

His mouth twisted derisively. 'If it's flattery you want, Jaz, you're talking to the wrong man!'

'Somehow I thought as much,' she returned dryly before moving out to the kitchen.

Why on earth couldn't Dennis, Barbara and Madelaine have kept their thoughts to themselves? she fumed inwardly as she clattered about the kitchen preparing coffee and taking out the mugs to put it in. Wasn't her life difficult enough as it was, without having Beau Garrett on her case?

'Were the vicar and his wife your father's or your mother's parents?'

The mug she was holding wobbled precariously in her hand, almost falling, although she managed to retrieve it at the last minute, turning sharply to look at Beau as he completely dwarfed her tiny kitchen. She hadn't been aware of him entering the room, abstractly wondering how such a big man managed to move so silently. Not that it mattered; he was here now, and the small confines of the room made his presence all the more palpable.

She gave him a puzzled frown. 'Why do you ask?'

He shrugged. 'Just making conversation.'

Her frown deepened; somehow she didn't think Beau was a man to make idle 'conversation'... 'My mother's,' she answered slowly.

He nodded, as if she had just confirmed something. 'I somehow couldn't see the transition of the son of a vicar into a gardener,' he explained ruefully.

Jaz stared at him for several seconds, and then she burst into derisive laughter. He couldn't see how the son of a vicar had become a professional gardener? Then he wouldn't have understood her mother, the daughter of a vicar, at all!

Beau gave her a searching look. 'Did I say something funny...?'

She sobered, slowly shaking her head. 'Not really.

But what do you think children of vicars should become? More vicars?'

He moved to lean back against one of the cupboards. 'I've never really thought about it before,' he admitted. 'It just seemed a strange choice.'

Jaz found the fact that he had thought about it now rather disturbing. She didn't want Beau Garrett to have thoughts about her, or members of her family…

'What was it like being the granddaughter of a vicar?' Beau continued conversationally.

Except, once again, she didn't think Beau was a man who engaged in idle conversation…

'Wearing,' she admitted abruptly. 'My grandparents always expected me to be perfect,' she explained at his questioning look. 'In contrast, the other children in the village used to tease me a lot.' No point in adding that Sharon, the barmaid from the pub, had been one of the worst culprits.

Beau nodded. 'I can see how that might be a problem.'

A problem? At times it had been a nightmare. Made worse by the fact that, as her parents had always been so busy doing other things, she spent a lot of time at weekends and school holidays with her grandparents. They were well-meaning people, obviously loved their only grandchild—while at the same time not understanding her in the least!

'It could have been worse,' she dismissed with a shrug, picking up the tray of coffee things in preparation of returning to the other room.

Beau gave her a considering look, making no move to follow her. 'Could it…?'

'Of course.' She gave him an over-bright smile. 'Would you mind getting the door for me?'

'Of course,' he echoed mockingly, moving to open the sitting room door too. 'This is rather nice. Cosy,' he added appreciatively as she looked up at him enquiringly. 'Maybe I would have been better off in a cottage rather than that huge house.'

'Maybe you would have been better off staying in London,' Jaz came back tartly as she handed him a mug of black coffee, leaving it up to him to add milk and sugar.

His gaze narrowed. 'Why do you say that?'

She gave a dismissive laugh as she sat down in the armchair. 'You fit in here about as well as a tiger would in suburbia!' No harm in trying to turn the tables on him; she would like nothing better than not returning to the reason for his visit here this evening! 'All prevarication apart, Beau; why are you living here?' she added with deliberate challenge.

His eyes glittered silver. '"All prevarication apart", Jaz—mind you own business!'

She nodded. 'Somehow I thought you would say that.'

'Then why ask?' He shrugged.

She grimaced. 'Just wanted to see if I was right.'

He sat down on the sofa, adding milk but not sugar to his coffee. 'You still haven't answered my question, Jaz.'

Her brows rose. 'Which one?' she enquired—knowing exactly which one, but really not wanting to answer it.

It had been extremely difficult continuing to live here after her mother had run away so abruptly, for her grandparents, as well as her father and herself, and now that they were all gone there was only Jaz to remember—and be remembered!—for the scandal that had so rocked the village and its inhabitants.

She had no doubts that Dennis's rib-nudging, Barbara's gossipy approval, and Madelaine's well-meaning remarks were all connected to that scandal…

Beau's gaze was narrowed to icy slits. 'Why are you "poor Jaz"? Why was it "kind" of me to take you to the pub last night? And why does Madelaine think you "deserve" to find yourself a nice young man?'

Jaz was ready for him this time, giving a dismissive shake of her head, a noncommittal smile curving her lips. 'Unless I've lost the ability to count, that was three questions!'

His mouth tightened. 'Unless I'm mistaken, all with the same answer!' he returned forcefully.

He wasn't mistaken, but it was rather galling to know that he knew it too!

It had been years now since her mother had left, so many years Jaz herself no longer even thought about it. But not so the other people in the village, it seemed…

She gave a shrug of narrow shoulders. 'It's what happens when you've lived in a village all your life, when you were born here, grew up here. People think they have the right to pass comment on your private life.'

Beau didn't look in the least convinced by her answer. 'And what about Dennis's rib-nudging and innuendos?' he reminded pointedly. 'Was he passing comment on your private life, too?'

She had forgotten about Dennis's behaviour! Although she could easily guess the reason for them; no doubt Dennis thought like mother, like—

She sat forward suddenly, the colour fading from her cheeks, eyes deeply blue against that paleness.

No!

It couldn't be Dennis who had sent her that anonymous note! Could it...?

He could have a computer, most people seemed to nowadays. But even if he did, that didn't prove anything; what household didn't have a computer nowadays? Well...she didn't, for one, but that was another matter!

No, the thought had been hers, not Dennis's, although that didn't change the fact that he always made it obvious he believed her to be her mother's daughter, that most of the men in the village had at some time been warned off her for that very reason. Not that that was a deterrent to all men; in fact, the opposite, in some cases! Although she had given those few misguided men short shrift with the sharpness of her tongue, and mostly they just left her alone nowadays.

She gave another shrug. 'Dennis likes to think of himself as a man of the world,' she derided dismissively. 'And as that's obviously what you are...' She trailed off pointedly.

Beau was still looking at her with narrowed eyes. 'Why do I have the feeling that there's something you aren't telling me?'

Her eyes widened at his accusatory tone. 'There's a lot you aren't telling me, but you don't hear me complaining!'

He settled back comfortably into the armchair. 'What do you want to know?' He took a sip of his coffee.

When he put it like that—nothing!

'Okay.' He nodded decisively when she hadn't answered him after several seconds. 'Let's see.' He seemed to give it some thought. 'I'm thirty-nine years old. An only child. My parents are both still living. In Surrey, if you're really interested,' he added dryly. 'I went to boarding-school near Worcester, then on to Cambridge University, reading Politics—again, if you're interested.' He raised mocking brows. 'I decided against a political career in favour of journalism. I've worked in television for the last twelve years.'

Jaz looked at him expectantly, waiting for him to continue his 'resume'. And waited. And waited.

'Well?' she finally prompted frowningly.

'Well what?' He raised deliberately innocent brows.

She gave a frustrated sigh. 'That was a pretty useless exercise, wasn't it?'

He shrugged. 'About as helpful to what you really wanted to know as your own explanation was to me a few minutes ago, wouldn't you say?'

Touché, she silently acknowledged. This man really was too bright for his own—and anyone else's!—good.

'Maybe,' she conceded quietly. 'But your explanation didn't tell me why you are living here when your work is in London.'

A shutter came down over already hooded eyes, his expression grim now; he was no longer relaxed as he sat in the chair. 'Because it isn't,' he rasped harshly.

Jaz frowned. 'Isn't what?'

Beau gave her an impatient glance. 'My work. It isn't in London,' he added abruptly as she still looked blank.

She stared at him perplexedly for several long minutes, none the wiser for doing so. 'I don't under-stand.' She finally gave a shake of her head. 'Have they moved the television studio up here—?'

'Jaz, I may not have known you very long,' he cut in icily, 'but it's certainly long enough for me to know you are far from lacking in intelligence!'

Her cheeks flushed with pleasure at what was, coming from this man, most definitely a compliment. Even if it hadn't sounded like one!

'Yes, but—' She broke off, drawing in a sharp breath as another explanation presented itself.

Beau Garrett was the leading host of any chat show on any television station, had been for almost a decade, but as far as she was aware there hadn't been any new programmes since his accident four months ago...

He had assured her that the scar didn't 'bother' him, but that didn't mean that it didn't bother someone else...

Surely the television studio, in its infinite wisdom, hadn't decided to drop his programme just because he was no longer the perfect, handsome presenter he had once been?

CHAPTER EIGHT

'WHAT are you thinking now?'

Jaz glanced up to find Beau looking at her with narrowed eyes. She couldn't help it, found her own gaze
drawn to that livid scar that ran the length of his face.
It wasn't pretty, she accepted that, but its lividness
would fade in time, probably only leaving a silvery line
to mark its presence. In time… Which was probably
something they didn't give you in the world of television!

Were the general public, the people who watched his
television show, really that fickle? Didn't they—?

'Jaz?' Beau prompted harshly.

She gave him a startled look, having forgotten that
he was still waiting for an answer. But what could she
say that he wouldn't take exception to? That she thought
the people who had made the decision to drop his television show, just because he had a scar on his face,
were a lot of idiots? That she believed the English public had more intelligence than they were being given
credit for? All of that, given the circumstances, sounded
totally inadequate for the humiliation he must have gone
through after so much pain.

'Time I was going, I think,' Beau rasped, standing
up abruptly. 'Thanks for the coffee, Jaz—even if I can't
say the same for the conversation,' he added dryly.
'That, I'm sure you'll be happy to know, was a total
waste of my time!'

As had his own been! Oh, she knew a little more

about him personally now, his parents, his education, his early career, but none of that helped her to understand the man he was now.

Jaz stood up too. 'I'm sorry I couldn't be more helpful.'

Beau's features lightened into a smile, his gaze warmly appreciative. 'You aren't sorry at all,' he drawled ruefully.

She shrugged. 'Okay, so I'm not. It was still nice to see you.' Especially as she had been wondering all day how they were possibly going to face each other again after Beau had kissed her the evening before. In retrospect, it hadn't been as difficult as she had thought it would be. Mainly because Beau had made sure that it wasn't…

'Was it?' He raised dark brows skeptically. 'I'm afraid I wasn't very nice to you when we parted last night,' he added huskily, silver gaze searching now.

She had spoken too soon!

Her cheeks warmed at this reminder of something she was sure they would both rather forget.

Beau grimaced at her obvious embarrassment. 'It's no excuse, I know, but I'm afraid I'm not really—adapting too well.' He frowned darkly. 'I certainly shouldn't have taken my bad temper out on you.'

Jaz looked at him curiously. 'Adapting to what?'

His mouth twisted humourlessly. 'You don't miss much, do you, Jaz?' He shook his head. 'You're a very strange mixture of intelligence and innocence—'

'For innocence read naïvety!' she cut in scornfully.

'Not at all,' he said slowly, his gaze totally assessing. 'In fact, Jasmina Logan—'

'I thought I warned you against calling me that,' she reminded him forcefully, feeling the usual queasiness in the pit of her stomach that her full name always invoked. Her mother had been one of the people who had always insisted on calling her by her full name…

'So you did,' he acknowledged lightly, at the same time making no effort to finish his earlier statement. Much to Jaz's frustration… She would have liked to know what had come after 'in fact'. But it was obvious by the way Beau was replacing his empty mug on the tray, and moving towards the door, that the conversation was over as far as he was concerned.

He paused as he reached the sitting room door. 'I shall be going away for the weekend tomorrow afternoon, so if there's anything you need from me before I go…?'

He was going away? But he had only just arrived!

Who was she kidding? The sinking feeling in her stomach, at being informed Beau was going away for a few days, had nothing to do with the fact that he had only recently moved into the village—and everything to do with the fact that even though he had only been here a short time, she was going to miss him, going to miss the way he just called in here whenever he felt like it, the way he gave colour to her life after what seemed like years of grey.

Which wasn't something she particularly enjoyed acknowledging… The reason she felt that way was something she just wasn't going to think about!

She straightened, her expression deliberately noncommittal. 'No, there's nothing I can think of,' she dismissed with a lightness she was far from feeling.

Where was he going? Who was he going to see? His parents, who lived in Surrey? Or someone else…?

It didn't really matter; she simply didn't have the right to ask him any of those things—especially when she had just discovered that there were other questions she needed to answer herself!

How had this man's presence become so essential to her life in such a short space of time? More important, why had it?

'Jaz?' Beau was looking at her questioningly now, his expression quizzical.

She forced an over-bright smile, knowing by the way Beau's gaze narrowed that he was well aware it was forced. 'There's really nothing I need from you,' she assured him lightly.

His mouth twisted derisively. 'You really know how to wound a man, do you know that, Jaz?' he taunted.

'Ha ha,' she muttered dryly, knowing he was teasing her.

He laughed softly. 'Actually, Jaz, in view of the other marriage-minded women in the area, you're very good for my ego—there's no chance of it becoming over-inflated with you around to keep my feet firmly on the ground!'

Then he wasn't reading her at all! The truth was, she was aware of this man with every part of her, felt nerve-tinglingly alive whenever she was in his company.

Whereas he, it seemed, regarded her more as the little sister he had obviously never had.

Which was probably just as well…

She gave him a rueful grin. 'Any time!'

He grinned back. 'That's what I thought.' He nodded. 'I—hello; what's this?' He bent down to retrieve something off the mat just inside the front door.

'What is it?' Jaz prompted sharply, a terrible premonition creeping over her.

He turned with a shrug. 'Just a letter. Obviously from someone too mean to affix a stamp—hey!' he protested teasingly as Jaz snatched the white envelope out of his hand.

Jaz stared down at the envelope she now held. It was just like the last one; as Beau had already pointed out, had no stamp on it, the name and address printed on the front.

'What is it?' Beau prompted sharply.

Her hand tightened on the envelope even as she looked up at him with over-bright eyes. 'If I'm lucky it might be someone paying a bill,' she attempted to dismiss lightly, knowing she fell far short of succeeding, but not willing to discuss these letters with anyone. Least of all this man.

Because she now had a feeling it was her new friendship with Beau that was causing them to be sent in the first place!

It had to be; there was no other man she had been even remotely close enough to for that initial accusation to have been made. Goodness knows, in view of her having had dinner with Beau at the pub last night in full view of half the village, what this second letter was going to say!

Whatever it was, she certainly wasn't going to open the letter while Beau was still here!

She moved forward to open the front door. 'Have a nice weekend, Beau,' she said lightly.

'You too,' he answered distractedly, his frowning gaze still fixed on her face. 'Jaz—'

'Goodness, it's turned cold this evening, hasn't it?' She affected a shiver as if to emphasize her point.

'Does that mean you'll have to turn up your heating in the greenhouses or something?'

Her mouth twisted wryly. 'Or something.'

Beau looked up at the sky, clouds whisking across

the blackness. 'I believe snow was forecast for this weekend.'

'Oh, wonderful,' she said with feeling.

He chuckled softly. 'Not good for the plants?'

'Not good at all. Brr,' she gave a genuine shiver this time. 'Take care on the roads tomorrow,' she advised.

Beau winced. 'You sound like my mother now!'

'I don't think, with you around, that there's any chance of my ego becoming over-inflated, either!' she snapped indignantly; his mother, indeed!

'I think,' he began, at the same time reaching up to gently caress one of her creamy cheeks, pausing to look at her quizzically as she blushed.

Jaz moistened her lips with the tip of her tongue, unable to move away, held captive by the look of tenderness on Beau's normally arrogant features. 'You think…?' she finally prompted.

He seemed to snap out of whatever trance he had briefly lapsed into, straightening, his hand falling away from her cheek. 'I think your ego could do with a little inflating,' he informed her harshly. 'In fact, more than a little,' he added hardly.

Her eyes flashed deeply blue. 'You—'

'Jaz, anyone with eyes in their head can see you have an inferiority complex the size of a house,' he continued remorselessly. 'Quite why, I have no idea—'

'How dare you?' Jaz gasped, her previous confusion fading as anger took over. Just who did this man think he was? Some amateur psychologist? He had no right!

'But one thing I can assure you—I intend finding out!' he concluded grimly.

She became suddenly still, barely breathing as she stared at him apprehensively, the unopened letter in her hand feeling like a ton weight. 'What do you mean?' she finally managed huskily.

'Exactly what I said, Jaz,' he bit out tersely. 'There has to be a reason why half the village pities you and the other half looks on you with suspicion.' He gave a disgusted shake of his head.

That was exactly how she was looked on in the village! And it hadn't even taken this man a week to realize it...

Her mouth twisted scornfully. 'I think you have an overactive imagination—'

'Really?' he snapped. 'Well, we'll see, won't we?'

Jaz swallowed hard. 'What do you mean?'

Beau shrugged. 'I'm not really sure,' he admitted with hard self-derision. 'One thing is becoming very clear to me, though...' He scowled.

'Yes?' she prompted breathlessly, that letter seeming to be burning her fingers now.

He gave a humourless smile. 'I should have looked into village life a little more before buying into it,' he rasped. 'I thought London was a minefield of gossip and speculation, but it's nothing compared to this!'

Jaz gasped. 'I think you're being a little unfair—'

'Do you? In the circumstances, that's very generous of you.' He gave another disgusted shake of his head. 'I'm a relative stranger here, have been resident only a matter of days, and yet several people have already chosen to discuss you with me—'

'That isn't quite true,' she defended indignantly. 'Barbara, Betty and Madelaine's comments have all been kindly meant, and as for Dennis!' She gave a disgusted snort. 'He was a friend of my father's—'

'Then he should know better,' Beau said icily.

'Yes, he should,' she acknowledged impatiently. 'But

my father was very hurt by my mother's desertion of him—'

'And you weren't?' Beau prompted incredulously. 'You were what? Seventeen, I think you said. Just at the age when you needed a mother's love and guidance. But instead you seem to have received pity or prejudice—'

'You don't understand, Beau,' Jaz cut in wearily.

No, he didn't understand, because he didn't know the full story—and she had no intention of telling him, either!—but at the same time he was far too astute than was comfortable.

'No, I don't,' he accepted heavily. 'Both your parents are gone, your grandparents too, so why the hell do you still live here?'

Jaz stared at him. No one had ever asked her that before. But the answer, now that she had been asked, was that she didn't know.

Where else would she go? She had been born here, brought up here, didn't know anywhere else.

But was that enough reason to stay…?

She had never even given that question any thought before, had simply gone on, day after day, barely keeping the garden centre afloat, with no thought that she could do anything else…

'Think about it,' Beau advised harshly.

She gave a tight smile. 'I think that you should mind your own business! You're very free with your advice about what I should or shouldn't do, for someone who—' She broke off abruptly, chewing on her bottom lip as she realized exactly what she had been about to say.

'"Someone who"…?' Beau prompted softly.

Dangerously so, Jaz easily recognized with a wince.

But he had stung her just now with his contempt for what he obviously saw as her lack of backbone in moving away from here and making a life for herself elsewhere. He couldn't possibly know that it actually took more courage to stay here than to go!

She shook her head. 'Forget it,' she dismissed, not quite meeting that glittering silver gaze now.

He turned fully in the hallway to face her. 'No, I don't think that I will,' he ground out derisively. 'What totally erroneous explanation have you contrived in your head to account for my moving to Aberton? That was where that previous statement was going, wasn't it?' he prompted in the dangerously soft voice.

Jaz swallowed hard, knowing the guilty colour had warmed her cheeks. 'I—'

'Careful now, Jaz,' he warned tauntingly.

She shot him a resentful glare. 'You aren't on your television programme now, Mr Garrett,' she snapped defensively. 'In fact, you no longer seem to have—' She gasped as she realized exactly what she had been about to say. 'I'm sorry. I didn't mean—'

'Yes, you did,' Beau taunted icily, his expression arrogantly remote. 'But I have no intention of satisfying any of the gossips as to the reason why I moved here— including you! You're getting cold.' He coldly acknowledged her earlier statement as she gave another shiver.

Only this shiver had nothing to do with the cold outside and everything to do with the icy disdain emanating from Beau himself.

She shouldn't have said what she did, she acknowledged that, it was just that Beau seemed to have a way of evoking a response in her—both physically as well as verbally!—that she would rather not give.

'Yes,' she acknowledged evenly. 'Have a nice weekend,' she added softly.

He gave a mocking inclination of his head before stepping outside. 'You, too,' he drawled dismissively.

A lot of chance she had of doing that, when she had another of those letters—as yet unopened—clutched in her hand!

CHAPTER NINE

'BUT where would you go, Jaz?' Madelaine looked up at her concernedly, holding the teapot poised over the two delicate china teacups in her surprise at what Jaz had just said.

Jaz had called in to see the older woman on her way home from working on Beau Garrett's garden most of the day—at the same time doing her best to avoid so much as speaking to Dennis Davis as he continued to work on the roof—now feeling in need of a little feminine company, and advice, and Madelaine was about the only person she felt comfortable enough with to do that. It had the added factor that it was afternoon-tea time, and, despite Jaz's less-than-elegant appearance, Madelaine was only too pleased to share tea with her unexpected guest.

She had nothing but admiration for Madelaine, the older woman having moved here from London with her husband fifteen years ago, continuing to stay on here after he died. To Jaz, Madelaine was everything that was elegant and charming, living her life like that of the Lady of the Manor, her house filled with genuine antiques, a live-in housekeeper to cook and clean for her, her own appearance always impeccable, her clothes expensively chic.

Everything that Jaz wasn't, in fact!

She shrugged now, accepting the cup of tea Madelaine had poured for her. 'I haven't really got that far in my thinking,' she answered the other woman's question. 'It's just that… The garden centre barely survives, as you know. The landscape gardening is pretty much the same, and Ted Soames—' the farmer whose son was to marry Sharon in three weeks' time! '—has always wanted to add the land to his already impressive farm, and—someone suggested that it might be a good idea for me to move away from here.' She grimaced.

Madelaine bent forward to pick up a plate and offer her one of the home-made scones provided by the housekeeper and covered in cream and jam, her smile teasing as she looked across at Jaz. 'And could this "someone" possibly be Beau Garrett?' she prompted, blonde brows raised speculatively.

Jaz could feel herself blushing, but it wasn't for the reason Madelaine was bound to think; the blush to her cheeks was caused by anger! The more she had thought over Beau's remarks to her the previous evening the angrier she had become, to the point that she wished now she had finished her own cutting remark.

Who did he think he was, challenging her in that way, especially when he seemed to have meekly accepted having his television show dropped in that way and crawled away with his 'tail between his legs'?

'The two of you seem to have become—quite close in the last week?' Madelaine added warmly.

Jaz's mouth firmed. 'Not at all. As you know, I'm working for him at the moment.' The whole village would know that by now!

Madelaine gave a husky laugh. 'My dear girl, I'm sure you must realize that everyone is agog with the knowledge that the two of you had dinner together the other evening!'

'It was hardly dinner—we merely had a pub meal together,' Jaz defended impatiently. Although it was the first time she had eaten any sort of meal out for longer than she could remember…

'You don't have to explain yourself to me.' Madelaine reached out and squeezed her hand reassuringly. 'I have been quite strong in my disapproval of the gossip, I do assure you.' She frowned. 'It's because it's Beau Garrett, of course,' she sighed.

Jaz gave a disgusted shake of her head. 'He's just a man, like any other.'

Madelaine gave her a look of girlish speculation. 'Surely not, Jaz?' she drawled.

Well…okay, Beau Garrett wasn't like any other man she had ever met before—or was ever likely to meet, either. She just wasn't feeling very kindly disposed towards him at the moment.

'He's far too old for me to be in the least interested in him in a romantic way,' she told the older woman firmly. 'And the thought of him being interested in me—in any way!—is ludicrous!' she added, with a twinge of insecurity.

'My dear Jaz, you underestimate yourself, as usual.' Madelaine shook her head reprovingly before taking a delicate sip of tea from the china cup, very beautiful today in a cream silk blouse and chocolate-coloured silk trouser suit, the chunky jewellery she wore not of the fake kind.

In fact, the two women were an unlikely pair to have formed a friendship, and yet Jaz was more comfortable with Madelaine than with anyone else, knew that she had no secrets from this woman.

'I don't think so.' She looked down pointedly at the over-large dungarees she had worn to work in today, another old jumper of her father's worn beneath them for warmth, in a particularly ugly shade of green that did nothing for her at all, and which she wasn't sure had done anything for him, either; where on earth had her father found these awful jumpers?

Madelaine gave her a considering look. 'You don't make the most of yourself, that's your problem. Now if I could just persuade you to come to London with me on one of my trips and have your hair professionally trimmed, your face professionally made up too, and you let me take you to a rather lovely store—'

'Stop right there,' Jaz told the other woman laughingly. 'For one thing I don't have the money to do any of those things—'

'It's your birthday soon, I could—'

'No, thank you, Madelaine,' Jaz cut in firmly, knowing exactly what the other woman was going to suggest; Madelaine was one of the most generous people she had ever met. 'It isn't just a case of not being able to afford them,' she continued ruefully. 'I would feel stupid—self-conscious,' she amended as Madelaine looked bemused. 'It wouldn't be me,' she concluded flatly.

'But it could become you,' the older woman insisted reasoningly. 'You have such lovely hair, Jaz. And your bone structure is—'

'Please stop!' Jaz actually laughed out loud now. 'I only wanted your opinion on my idea of selling up and moving,' she reminded teasingly, knowing the other woman meant well, but also knowing she would be most uncomfortable with this 'make-over' Madelaine was suggesting.

The other woman gave it some thought. 'I don't suppose it's such a bad idea,' she murmured consideringly. 'It depends on your reasons for doing it, of course… Jaz, has something happened?' She frowned concernedly.

Jaz stiffened slightly in her chair, at the same time making every effort to keep her expression noncommittal.

Had something happened!

The second letter, also anonymous, which she had opened the previous evening as soon as she'd been sure Beau had definitely gone, was even more upsetting than the first one had been. 'Find your own man, and not someone else's, like your mother did'.

Again, Jaz had been sure the writer had to be referring to Beau Garrett—there simply was no other man she had been even remotely close to!—and the implication was that Beau was already committed elsewhere, maybe already married. But Beau had already assured her that he wasn't, so that part of that single line didn't make any sense to her. The rest of it, concerning her mother, made altogether too much sense!

'No,' she assured Madelaine stiltedly. 'Nothing has happened. I just—I never even considered moving before. And now that I have…well, I can't understand why I didn't think of it before. It's perfect, a new start, away from here and everything that happened—' She broke off awkwardly. 'I think maybe I just need a fresh start, Madelaine,' she concluded huskily.

Madelaine's smile was wholly sympathetic to what Jaz wasn't saying, the other woman having lived in the village long enough to know that Jaz's life so far certainly hadn't been a bed of roses. 'The idea does have some merit.' She nodded frowningly. 'I'm just not sure it's a good idea for anyone to move completely away from things that are familiar. Charles and I did that when we moved here, and I adapted quite well—in fact, I can't imagine living anywhere else now,' she acknowledged ruefully. 'But it doesn't always work out that way,' she warned concernedly. 'What would you do about a job, for instance, and somewhere to live?'

Jaz gave a rueful smile. 'I could work in a garden centre for someone else—and earn regular money for a change! As for somewhere to live—there should be enough money from the sale of the cottage and land for me to buy myself a small cottage somewhere.'

Madelaine gave her an admiring look. 'Well, I can see you've obviously given this some thought. And I can't say it's a bad idea, but—I will miss you if you go, Jaz,' she added wistfully.

Madelaine's friendship was one of the few things she would miss if she went ahead with this idea to sell up and move away. But the other woman was slightly wrong in assuming Jaz had given this idea a lot of thought; most of her plans—amazingly!—seemed to have come together in her head as she was actually talking.

Madelaine eyed her teasingly now. 'Are you sure Beau Garrett doesn't have something to do with this?'

Jaz stiffened. 'Very sure,' she bit out more forcefully than she intended, forcing a smile as the other woman's eyes widened slightly at her vehemence.

'Hmm,' Madelaine murmured speculatively. 'Well, we'll see, shall we?'

'No, honestly, Madelaine,' she assured the other woman decisively. 'I have this job to finish for him, and after that I probably won't see him again.'

'I wouldn't be too sure of that,' the other woman murmured enigmatically.

Jaz would—in future she intended keeping any relationship with Beau Garrett on a purely businesslike footing; the man was altogether too fond of passing personal remarks for her liking!

*   *   *

'Ready?'

Jaz stared dazedly at Beau Garrett as he stood on her doorstep, wearing a heavy black coat over what looked like a black dinner suit and bright white shirt and bow-tie, rubbing his hands together in order to keep them warm.

She blinked. 'Ready for what?' But she had a feeling she already knew!

Madelaine had telephoned this morning and invited Jaz over for dinner this evening, explaining she had guests staying for the weekend and had decided to invite a few people over to meet them—as if Madelaine had ever needed an excuse to throw a dinner party! The other woman thrived on social occasions, and, when there weren't any, contrived to make her own.

Jaz had been only too willing to accept the other woman's invitation; the garden centre was always busy on a Sunday, and the thought of cooking dinner at the end of her busy day wasn't a pleasant one.

So instead she had taken a leisurely bath after locking up for the day, taking her one good dress from the ward-robe, the same dress she had worn to Madelaine's drinks party the previous week, her 'little black dress', suitable for any occasion. She had bought it while at college, and it was getting old now, but the straight, short-sleeved, knee-length style was classic, and so wouldn't date. Besides, there was nothing else for her to wear!

Beau Garrett was looking at her admiringly, her hair newly washed and curling silkily down her spine, wear-ing foundation and lip gloss this evening, very conscious of her legs beneath the short dress, too.

'Madelaine's, of course,' he easily confirmed her suspicions as to his being one of Madelaine's guests this evening too.

Jaz frowned. 'But I thought—you said you were away for the weekend,' she reminded him abruptly, desperately trying to re-evaluate this evening in her mind.

She had been expecting to meet several of the sophisticated friends that Madelaine often invited from London, was already acquainted with quite a few of them, but she certainly hadn't expected Beau Garrett to be amongst their number.

'I was,' he replied unhelpfully. 'And I can see that you're ready to go.' He nodded his appreciation of her changed appearance. 'Do you want to get a coat so we can be on our way? They were right about the snow,' he added with a grimace at the sprinkling of snow that covered the frozen ground.

Yes, they had been, a light dusting of it still covering the ground, the evening air frosty to say the least. But that wasn't her main concern at the moment.

'Madelaine telephoned and asked me, because of the weather, if I would mind collecting you on the way,' Beau supplied dryly as he seemed to guess what her 'concern' was. 'There's no point in both of us driving when we don't have to,' he added dismissively.

No, there wasn't—but Jaz had a definite feeling that wasn't Madelaine's prime motive behind the telephone call; she had never thought of the other woman as a matchmaker, but she had a feeling that was exactly what the other woman was being by throwing her and Beau together in this way!

'Come on, Jaz, get a move on,' Beau chided impatiently. 'It's cold out here!'

Yes, it was, and she was being a little ungrateful, in the circumstances, by keeping him standing outside on the doorstep. It was just that she was a little taken aback to see him at all...

'Come inside while I get my coat,' she invited stilt-edly, turning to run back up the stairs and collect her winter coat from the wardrobe. It was bright red, and ankle-length, and she had bought it on impulse five years ago, only to discover it was one of those coats that never wore out; she looked like Mrs Christmas in it!

Beau nodded his approval as she hurried back down the stairs. 'Red suits you,' he supplied as she eyed him suspiciously.

'Thank you,' she accepted stiltedly as she walked out through the door he was holding open for her.

Beau chuckled softly as he followed behind her. 'You are the least gracious woman I have ever known when it comes to receiving a compliment,' he explained mockingly as she gave him a backward glance.

Jaz gave him a glare. 'Maybe that's because where you're concerned I'm never sure it is a compliment!'

She had barely finished speaking when she felt her arm grasped as Beau turned her to face him in the dark-ness, the clear moonlight illuminating the frown on his brow.

He looked down at her searchingly. 'What's wrong, Jaz?' he finally prompted slowly.

'It's cold,' she tried to shake off his hand and only succeeded in encouraging him to tighten his grip. 'If we don't leave now we're going to be late,' she pointed out impatiently, wishing he would stop looking at her in that totally focused way; it made her feel as if he could look deep inside her, somehow, and read her deepest thoughts. Which, at the moment, would not be a good idea!

For one thing, she was still a little shaken by his presence here at all. For another, he looked breathtakingly handsome in the tailored suit and shirt, and as for the smell of his aftershave…that was doing very strange things to her pulse rate!

Beau shook his head. 'Ten minutes one way or the other isn't going to make much difference,' he shrugged. 'So what's happened, Jaz?' His gaze narrowed piercingly.

She made an impatient movement. 'Why does everyone keep asking me that at the moment?'

'Probably because at least some of us are concerned about you!' he came back decisively. 'And by "everyone", I take it you mean Madelaine and myself?' he added dryly. 'No one else in this place seems to give a damn what happens to you.'

Jaz felt the warmth enter her cheeks. 'You have absolutely no basis on which to—Oh!' she gasped before Beau claimed her mouth in a crushing kiss.

Jaz melted. Her lips softened and moved beneath his, her body curving into his hardness, every part of her, it seemed, becoming fluid.

She wanted this man. The last few days of telling herself he was arrogant, and opinionated, and just far too full of himself all melted away as he continued to kiss her, his arms about her now as he sipped and tasted the warmth of her lips.

Beau's expression was grim when he finally lifted his head and held her in front of him by her upper arms, eyes glittering silver in the moonlight. 'Don't I?' he ground out harshly, giving an impatient shake of his head. 'Has anyone, in your entire life, shown you any kindness?'

Jaz stiffened as if he had struck her, her eyes wide blue pools in the paleness of her face. 'How dare you—'

'How dare I?' he repeated angrily. 'I'll tell you why I dare—'

'No, I don't believe you will,' Jaz cut in coldly, pulling out of his grasp, the thickness of her coat preventing it from actually bruising her, her moment of madness over as quickly as it had begun; the last thing she wanted from this man was pity! 'You're far too fond of "telling" people your opinion,' she bit out disgustedly as she stepped firmly away from him. 'And I would prefer it if you didn't kiss me again, either,' she added icily.

'Would you?' Beau eyed her challengingly. 'And what if I can't stop myself?'

Her eyes flashed deeply blue. 'Then I would advise you to resist the impulse,' she said warningly.

He continued to look at her for several long seconds, and then he gave a shrug of his shoulders. 'Maybe,' he drawled derisively. 'It really depends on how much provocation you give me,' he added tauntingly before moving to unlock the Range Rover so they could both get inside.

In future, Jaz decided indignantly, she didn't intend giving him any provocation to do anything.

Anything at all…!

CHAPTER TEN

'BEAU—darling!'

Jaz was almost knocked off her feet as a woman swept past her in a direct path to Beau, briefly enveloping Jaz in a wave of her heady perfume, the woman letting out another squeal of delight before she launched herself into Beau's arms.

Waiting arms, Jaz noted with some disgruntlement as she turned to look at them. Although why she should feel that way after the disagreement the two of them had had before coming here, she had no idea. Well…she had some idea—she just wasn't willing to probe into it too deeply when Beau was being lingeringly kissed on the mouth by the tall, lissom blonde!

'Camilla,' Beau greeted dryly—when he had his lips free to say anything!

'The one and only,' the beautiful blonde acknowledged perkily, slipping her arm possessively into the crook of his as she smiled up at him.

At the same time managing to look as if she would like to eat him instead of dinner, Jaz decided frowningly.

They had barely got into Madelaine's house, Jaz handing her coat to the young girl from the next village who came to help out whenever Madelaine was entertaining—she was the daughter of Dennis Davis's 'friend', Jaz believed—before this woman Camilla had come bursting out of Madelaine's elegant sitting room to launch herself at Beau.

Not that he seemed to be in the least upset by this enthusiastic greeting, grinning widely at the other woman now—at the same time seeming to forget that Jaz was even there.

Jaz opened her shoulder bag and took out a tissue. 'Here,' she held it out to him. 'That shade of lipstick does nothing for you,' she informed him waspishly as he looked at her enquiringly.

Camilla was the one to take the tissue out of Jaz's hand, laughing softly as she slowly wiped the lip gloss from Beau's mouth, at the same time managing to make it look like an act of even deeper intimacy than the original kiss had been!

I give up, Jaz decided impatiently as she turned her back on the other couple and moved into the sitting room, her movements stiff and uncoordinated as she tried to come to terms with the feelings coursing through her.

Jealousy.

It was an emotion she had never known before, and yet she had no doubts that what she was feeling—the anger and resentment, at the same time as a slight but definite nausea—were due to seeing the woman Camilla kissing Beau in that familiar way.

It was not only painful, but humiliating; how could she possibly feel jealous over someone who made her so angry one moment and so softly compliant to his kisses the next? Quite easily, when she was falling in love with him, came the immediate answer.

Jaz stopped in her tracks. Falling in love with Beau Garrett? Had she completely lost her mind? What—?

'Jaz!' Madelaine greeted warmly as she crossed the room. 'And have you seen— Ah,' she gave a rueful grimace as Beau and the beautiful Camilla entered the room together at that moment, turning concernedly to look at Jaz. 'I'm so sorry,' she sighed, at the same time touching Jaz's arm consolingly.

Jaz gave the other woman a startled look. 'What on earth for?'

Madelaine shook her head. 'I had no idea that Camilla even knew Beau until a few minutes ago when I happened to mention he was one of the guests invited to dinner.' She gave another grimace, self-derisive this time. 'So much for "the feather in my cap"!' She turned to look over to where Camilla was determinedly keeping Beau in conversation. 'It looks as if we've all lost out this evening; Camilla doesn't look as if she's about to release Beau's attention any time soon!' She gave a rueful shake of her head.

Jaz determinedly kept her gaze away from the other couple, not even going to give Beau the satisfaction of noticing him now that they were at Madelaine's, the sitting room crowded with eight or nine other guests. 'Madelaine, I realize what you were doing by asking Beau to pick me up and bring me here this evening,' she chided gently. 'But you really do have the wrong impression concerning—concerning the two of us,' she finished firmly.

Madelaine gave her a teasing smile. 'I was just trying to be helpful.'

'I know,' Jaz sighed. 'But as you can see—' at last she did turn and look at the still-chatting Beau and Camilla now '—he's way out of my league!'

'Don't be silly, Jaz,' Madelaine patted her hand in rebuke. 'A man like Beau soon tires of vacuously beautiful women like darling Camilla—fond as I am of her.'

Vacuous or not, Camilla's idea of a 'little black dress'—a short, strapless affair that clung in all the right places—made Jaz feel as conservatively dressed as a nun!

'Never mind,' Madelaine dismissed briskly. 'There's plenty of time yet.'

'Plenty of time for wh—?'

'Come and say hello to the Booths,' Madelaine cut in briskly on Jaz's query, already pulling her in the direction of the vicar and his pretty young wife as they stood chatting with another couple near the fireplace.

Jaz was only too pleased to stop and chat to the Booths as Madelaine rushed off to greet another arriving guest, the couple they had been talking to having wandered off to join another group after the initial introductions.

She had always liked the Booths, Robert tall and distinguished-looking, and aged in his mid-forties, Betty small and blonde, and only a year or so older than Jaz herself.

On first acquaintance the couple seemed an oddly matched pair, but over the last year or so since the Booths moved to Aberton Jaz had come to realize that Betty, although appearing fluffy and disorganized, was in fact the one that kept the vicarage and Robert's many parish duties running so smoothly.

'Isn't this wonderful?' Betty beamed now, looking very pretty in a pale blue dress. 'Sundays are always such a busy day for us; it was so nice of Madelaine to telephone this afternoon and invite us here to dinner after evening service.'

Jaz, having had a grandfather who was a vicar, was well aware of the many demands made of them, and could well appreciate that Betty welcomed this change in routine. Robert was a little harder to fathom, tending to hold himself slightly aloof on such occasions, although he was obviously quite happy to indulge his pretty wife in this unexpected treat.

'I feel the same way,' Jaz smiled sympathetically. 'The garden centre is always busy at the weekends, too.'

'I'm glad to hear it,' Beau drawled as he joined them. 'I brought you over a glass of champagne,' he said in answer to Jaz's questioning look, holding out the bubbling glass of wine.

She blinked her surprise at his being here at all, not having expected to see too much more of him this evening. What on earth had he done with the beautiful Camilla?

His mouth twisted derisively as he followed her searching gaze. 'Camilla has rejoined her fiancé,' he explained mockingly.

Poor fiancé, was Jaz's first thought; she wouldn't have been too happy herself at having anyone she was engaged to greeting another woman in that effusive way!

'Talking of which...' Beau continued softly '...it wasn't very polite of you to just desert your dinner partner in that abrupt way.'

'My dinner partner!' Jaz's eyes had widened indignantly.

Beau turned to the other couple. 'I'm afraid I'm not one of those modern men who arrives with a woman and then only meets up with her again when it's time to leave,' he confided conversationally.

'Quite right,' Robert nodded approvingly.

'I can't say I would be too happy with that.' Betty linked her arm through Robert's in an affectionate gesture.

Neither would Jaz have been—if that had truly been the case. Which it wasn't!

'Well, excuse me—'

'You're excused,' Beau cut in smoothly on Jaz's indignant outrage. 'Try the champagne; it's delicious.' He held the glass out to her once again, grey eyes laughing at her obvious desire to tell him exactly what she thought of him, while at the same time being slightly hamstrung by the Booths' presence.

She took the proffered glass of champagne, taking a restorative gulp—anything to stop her from completely embarrassing herself by giving in to the impulse she had to slap that taunting grin off Beau's arrogantly handsome face.

'I do so love these formal dinners.' Betty was the one to lightly fill in the silence that seemed to have descended. 'Although I don't envy Madelaine's cook having to feed so many of us!' she added ruefully.

There were at least a dozen people in the room, most of them friends of Madelaine's from London, with only the Booths and Jaz living locally—the major, she noted, was conspicuous by his absence—but she didn't doubt that Madelaine's housekeeper would cope, as she always did on these occasions, quite comfortably.

'Do excuse us, won't you?' Robert prompted politely as Madelaine beckoned from across the room, obviously wanting to introduce the other couple to the man she was talking to.

'Go ahead.' Beau nodded, smiling.

Jaz waited barely long enough for the other couple to leave before turning glaringly on Beau. 'What do you mean "dinner partner"?' she demanded.

He raised dark brows. 'You arrived with me, didn't you?'

'Yes. But—'

'We are here to eat dinner, aren't we?' Beau prompted smoothly.

She sighed. 'Yes. But—'

'And I have no doubt that Madelaine—God bless her matchmaking heart!—will have seated us next to each other at the table?' he continued determinedly.

Jaz grimaced. 'Probably.' God bless her matchmaking heart!

He shrugged. 'Then what else do we have to do to be classed as dinner partners?'

In all honesty, she wasn't absolutely sure—all she did know was that they were not here as a couple!

'Beau, you know very well that you just gave me a lift here.' She at least tried to make some sense of the situation. 'That does not put you under any obligation to spend the rest of the evening, or indeed, part of it, with me.'

He raised dark brows. 'Doesn't it?'

'No!' She could barely contain her impatience now.

'Hmm.' He pursed his lips thoughtfully. 'Well, as far as I'm concerned, it puts you under obligation to spend the rest of the evening, not part of it, with me.'

Jaz looked at him frowningly, her searching gaze being met with a look of bland innocence. Which was not an emotion she in the least connected to Beau!

She gave him a derisive smile. 'Wouldn't that cramp your style a little?'

'Probably a lot,' he conceded lightly. 'But as there's no one else here that I particularly want to spend time with, it looks as if you're stuck with me.'

From the envious looks Jaz had been receiving from the other women in the room since Beau had joined her, she had a feeling she was the only woman here who didn't want to be 'stuck with him'. And her reasons for feeling that way were completely her own!

Could she really be falling in love with this man? It would be an act of madness if she were. But then, when had she ever claimed she was a sane and reasonable person? Never, as far as she was aware. Well, falling in love with Beau proved it—she wasn't either of those things!

'What?'

She gave a guilty start as she realized Beau was looking at her with narrowed eyes, although from the abruptness of his query he didn't have any idea what she had been thinking about so intensely. Thank goodness!

'Nothing.' She gave a dismissive shake of her head, turning away from him deliberately to look at the other people gathered in the room. 'Do you usually go to a lot of dinner parties like this one?' The three locals apart, they were a glittering bunch of people, the women beautiful, the men all handsome, Jaz recognizing a couple of the faces from television.

Beau gave a noncommittal grimace. 'Not in the last couple of weeks or so, no.'

Since he had moved to Aberton...

'And not that many when I lived in London, either— if I could possibly avoid it,' he said hardly.

'I find that hard to believe,' Jaz commented. After all, didn't part of what he did—what he had done?— involve meeting people at social gatherings of this sort?

Beau gave a decisive shake of his head. 'I wouldn't be here tonight either if Madelaine hadn't told me you were coming,' he added huskily.

Jaz turned sharply to look at him, but, apart from the laughter still lurking in those silver-grey eyes, she could read nothing from his expression. 'And why should that have made a difference?' She tried to keep her own tone as noncommittal, but knew by the way her voice rose slightly in tenor that she hadn't succeeded.

But why should her presence here have made a difference to whether or not Beau accepted Madelaine's dinner invitation? Unless he was attracted to her, possibly even falling in love with her too—

Now she was being utterly ridiculous! Half a glass of champagne was obviously half a glass too much! Because there was no way a sophisticated man like Beau was falling in love with her. If he felt anything towards her at all then it was pity. And she could do without that, thank you...

'Forget I even asked that,' she told him hastily as Madelaine announced that dinner was ready to be served, Jaz moving to put her champagne glass down on top of the fireplace; no more wine for her this evening, not if it was going to make her have wild thoughts like her previous one!

Beau reached out and put a lightly restraining hand on her arm. 'What if I don't want to forget it?' he prompted huskily.

Jaz couldn't quite meet his gaze, looking somewhere across his left shoulder. 'Just accept that I do and leave it at that, hmm,' she said waspishly.

He seemed to give the idea some thought before giving a slow shake of his head. 'No, I don't think that I will. In fact, we're definitely going to get back to this later,' he promised softly.

Much, much later, if Jaz had anything to do with it. And she did.

Didn't she...?

CHAPTER ELEVEN

'YOU can stop gnashing your teeth now, Jaz,' Beau chuckled softly in the darkness beside her as he drove the two of them away from Madelaine's house later that evening.

No, she couldn't. If she stopped gnashing her teeth she would start talking. And if she started talking, there was no telling what she might say!

It hadn't been the worst evening she had ever spent in her life—that award had to go to a date she had had when she was eighteen!—but it had certainly been far from the most enjoyable, either.

Beau had been correct in his assumption that Madelaine would seat the two of them next to each other, unfortunately Madelaine had also inadvertently seated Camilla on Beau's other side. And Camilla wasn't a woman who liked to share male attention with anyone—least of all with someone she considered nothing more than a country bumpkin. As she obviously did Jaz!

'Are you sure Gerald is her fiancé?' she snapped, not having seen much evidence of it the last couple of hours, as Camilla completely ignored the other man and concentrated her considerable charms on Beau.

'Well, he is, and he isn't. Camilla is more of a smokescreen really,' Beau answered slowly. 'If you know what I mean?'

'No, I—' She broke off, staring at Beau in the semi-darkness. 'Are you telling me that Gerald is—that he's—'

'Yep,' Beau confirmed her suspicions. 'Unfortunately his father—who happens to be head of Burnet Television—doesn't know, and wouldn't approve if he did. Which is why Gerald decided he needed a fiancée for a while just to allay any suspicions his father may get concerning his marriageless state. A female fiancée, of course,' he added dryly.

'Of course,' Jaz acknowledged just as dryly.

She would never have guessed of Gerald's lack of interest in the opposite sex; he was extremely good-looking, and she had found him thoroughly charming, on the single occasion the two of them had chance to talk.

'But don't be misled into thinking Gerald is using Camilla,' Beau continued. 'This arrangement is just as convenient for her, I can assure you.' He shrugged dis-missively.

Jaz's eyes widened incredulously. 'You aren't telling me that Camilla's gay too?'

'No, I'm not telling you that.' Beau gave a firm shake of his head as he began to chuckle again. 'As well as his father, Gerald has a number of important family con-nections in the world of television and films, and Camilla is an ambitious young lady. So she's helping him out by temporarily being his fiancée, and—'

'In return he's going to "help her out" with her career,' Jaz finished scornfully. 'It's all a little—false, isn't it?' She shook her head disgustedly. 'Not that I'm in the least interested in where his—interests lay,' she defended hastily. And she really wasn't. A person's sex-ual preferences were their own affair as far as she was concerned. 'It just seems rather contrived and a bit…exploitative,' she finished lamely.

She had spent the better part of the evening being jealous of a woman who was engaged to a man simply in the interest of furthering her career! Could it be that Camilla saw Beau as another man to be exploited?

'Clever girl,' Beau drawled ruefully after giving her a sideways glance. 'Yes, Camilla is an ambitious young lady all right. It's a pity she was wasting her time where I'm concerned,' he added hardly.

Jaz gave him a searching look. Did he mean Camilla was wasting her time because he just wasn't interested in her in that way? Or did he mean something else…?

His mouth thinned. 'As you've already guessed, I'm no longer involved in that world,' he bit out harshly.

As she had already guessed indeed. But she still wasn't sure whether it was by choice or necessity. Although from the few conversations they had had on the subject, she would say it was the latter…

'Anyway—' Beau straightened in the driving seat '—Madelaine has had words with me this evening concerning putting "ideas into your head".' He raised his dark brows questioningly.

Jaz looked at him blankly for several seconds, a frown marking her brow as she suddenly wondered whether Madelaine, dear as she was, could possibly have totally embarrassed her by warning Beau not to play with her emotions. Please, no…

'Yes, apparently you've discussed the idea of leaving the area with her,' Beau continued conversationally. 'After telling me to mind my own business for even mentioning it!'

Jaz could feel the warm colour in her cheeks. 'You didn't just "mention" it—you taunted me with it!' she returned sharply. 'And, yes, I may have discussed it with Madelaine, but that's really none of your business either, is it?' she added rudely.

He gave an unconcerned shrug. 'That really depends on whether or not I choose to make it my business, now doesn't it?'

Jaz gave an indignant gasp. 'No, it does not!' She glared at him in the darkness. 'When you first—made the suggestion,' she tautly amended her initial accusation, 'I thought it was totally ridiculous. But on thinking about it, I decided perhaps it may be worth considering.'

'And?'

'I'm still considering,' she snapped.

'I'd get more joy from watching grass grow than trying to get a straight answer out of you!' he came back just as snappily.

'Be my guest,' Jaz scorned. 'You'll find it grows very slowly this time of year!'

'You know, Jaz,' he said slowly, a smile starting to curve those sculpted lips, 'being with you is never boring.'

'I'm glad I'm good for something—even if it is only alleviating your boredom!' she returned waspishly.

Although secretly she was rather 'glad'; if Beau didn't find being with her boring, that was at least something positive!

'Invite me in for coffee.'

Jaz turned to him frowningly, at the same time realizing he had brought the Range Rover to a halt in her driveway, that he was now turned slightly in his seat as he waited for her reply.

She moisted her lips, not sure that inviting him in—for coffee or anything else!—was a particularly good idea; every time she had done that so far Beau had ended up kissing her.

Maybe it was a good idea, after all!

She liked being kissed by Beau. Perhaps liked it a little too much?

'Go on, Jaz, invite me in, live dangerously for once in your life,' Beau murmured huskily.

Living dangerously was not an option in her life at the moment, it only seemed to lead to trouble. And with the arrival of those two anonymous letters, she already had enough of that.

She drew in a slow breath. 'Actually, I'm a little tired—'

'Then I'll make the coffee.'

'It's Monday tomorrow—'

'I don't mind if you arrive a little late for work.'

Her brow creased into a frown of frustration as he easily knocked down every barrier she put in his way. 'I don't particularly want a cup of coffee—'

'Okay, let's forget the coffee, and just invite me in anyway.'

That rather defeated the whole basis of her objections!

'Jaz.' Beau reached out to lightly cup her cheek in his hand, his thumb moving to lightly caress the soft pout of her lips. 'Invite me in,' he prompted evenly, his eyes glowing in the darkness.

She swallowed again, feeling the rush of adrenalin through her body created just by having Beau touch her in this way. If he came into the cottage, where would it all stop? If it stopped at all!

'I—'

'I'm coming in,' he told her firmly, his hand falling

back to his side, and he turned and got out of the vehicle before she could say another word.

Because he had known that she was about to say a determined no to his coming inside! How could he help but know? She hadn't exactly been overwhelming in her enthusiasm so far!

She joined him on the snow-covered driveway, deliberately not looking at him as she searched through her handbag for her key, having left the small outside light on earlier so that she would be able to see what she was doing when she returned.

'You look like a scared rabbit!' Beau's voice bit harshly into the surrounding darkness.

She raised her head to glare at him, having at last located her door key. 'Maybe that's because I feel like a "scared rabbit"!' she snapped impatiently.

He became very still, eyes narrowed to silver slits. 'Do I frighten you?'

'Yes! No!' she amended irritably.

His expression was grim. 'Make your mind up, Jaz; is it yes or no?' As if by instinct, rather than design, his hand moved to the scar on his face.

She could repeat yes, and knew that he would leave then, knew by the way his fingers ran absently down that livid scar on this cheek that he would do so completely misunderstanding the reason for her fear. But could she really do that? Could she wound him in that way, even to save herself? The answer to that was a resounding no!

'It's no,' she sighed impatiently. 'It isn't you that frightens me, it's—' She broke off awkwardly, not comfortable with admitting it was fear of her own response to him that made her so reluctant to be alone with him again.

But wasn't she alone with him now? Couldn't Beau just as easily kiss her here and now, and still be able to melt her bones to water, her resistance to quivering jelly? Of course he could, but he was hardly likely to make love to her out here in the icy cold, the ground still covered with snow, whereas once they were alone in the cottage…

Beau moved so that he was standing directly in front of her, so close they almost touched. Almost. 'Jaz, do you believe me when I say I would never do anything to hurt you?' he prompted huskily, his gaze easily capturing and holding hers.

She was having trouble breathing, her knees were knocking together; one of which might kill her, the other leave her floundering in the snow at his feet— wouldn't that hurt her?

And if Beau made love to her—as the intensity of his gaze promised that he wanted to do!—and then left her, wouldn't that hurt her?

She gave a dazed shake of her head. 'You wouldn't mean to, maybe, but you would do it anyway.'

He continued to look at her for several long seconds, and then he gave a sigh of frustration, whether at her indomitableness, or because he knew she spoke the truth, Jaz wasn't completely sure.

He gave a shake of his head. 'You're right, I wouldn't mean to,' he repeated huskily.

She nodded, eyes deeply blue with emotion. 'But you would do it anyway,' she finished gruffly.

He gave a pained frown, his gaze searching now on the paleness of her face. 'I would hope not,' he finally murmured. 'But, in all honesty, at this time of uncertainty in my life, the only thing I can be sure of is that I don't know!'

Whereas she, in a blaze of sudden insight, knew exactly what she wanted! She wanted this man, wanted him completely, knew with blinding clarity that her questioning of her emotions earlier had all been a waste of time—because she was in love with him.

The step Beau had just taken away from her she now took in his direction, knowing that the whole of this evening, since she had first opened the door three hours or so ago and felt that rush of pleasure at finding Beau there, had all been leading to this moment.

'Perhaps,' her voice was huskily emotional. 'Perhaps you just need someone to help you to know...' She stepped fully into his arms, standing on tiptoe to press her lips against his.

Beau stood unmoving for several awful seconds, and then his arms moved to pull her tightly against him, at the same time his lips opening to deepen the kiss she had so innocently begun.

Jaz melted into Beau's hardness, their bodies moulding together from her breasts to her thighs, her arms up about his shoulders now, her fingers laced into the dark thickness of the hair at his nape, their mouths fused in pleasure-filling intimacy.

Her breasts felt taut and tingling as she pressed close against him, a heat in her thighs that cried out to be assuaged, and all the time that kiss continued and continued!

She gasped as she felt Beau's hand on her breast beneath her coat, that gasp turning to a groan as his thumb-tip moved caressingly over the aroused tip, pleasure moving mercurially through her body, her legs once again feeling weak.

She ached, how she ached, her breath coming in ragged gasps as the heat engulfed her—

The headlights of a car, as it turned the corner past the cottage, shone blindingly in her face, acting as soberly as a bucket of cold water would have done, Beau obviously feeling that same chill of reason as he raised his head to look down at her.

She could read nothing from his gaze in those few brief seconds of sight before the car continued on its journey, taking those intrusive headlights with it. But just those few seconds were enough to show Jaz that whatever moment of emotional intimacy had just passed between the two of them, it was over now, Beau once more retreating behind that wall of aloofness he sometimes chose to adopt.

She straightened, forcing a teasing smile to her lips, at the same time hoping that Beau couldn't see the pain in her eyes. 'You see, I told you it wasn't a good idea!'

'And you were right,' he acknowledged harshly, stepping back from her abruptly before thrusting his hands into the pocket of his overcoat.

She nodded. 'I'll see you tomorrow, then,' she told him brightly, determined to wait until after he had left before letting the heated tears fall down her cheeks— as they threatened to do at any second.

'Probably,' he confirmed forcefully. 'Jaz—'

'Just go, Beau,' she encouraged huskily, knowing she couldn't stand here and listen to any explanations of his about 'not wanting to get involved'—she could already see the regret in his face, didn't need to hear the words too!

He gave a self-disgusted shake of his head. 'I don't want—'

'Will you please just go?' she repeated tautly, knowing she was balanced on a knife-edge of emotion—and threatening to tumble over the side at any moment! 'Just put this down to…misplaced curiosity.'

He frowned. 'Is that what this was?'

'Definitely,' Jaz confirmed firmly. 'And don't worry, it won't happen again.'

Beau let out his breath in a deep sigh. 'It isn't that I don't like you, Jaz—'

'Well I may be inexperienced, but even I could tell that!' she came back scornfully. A few minutes ago, their bodies pressed together from breast to thigh, Beau's arousal had been even more tangible than her own!

'Yes,' he acknowledged heavily. 'I'm just not sure— I may not stay on here, Jaz, and—' He gave an uncomfortable shrug.

He didn't have to tell her that if he went back to London, took up his career again, albeit perhaps in a different role from the one he had had for so long, there would be no place for Jaz in that life.

'You don't owe me any explanations, Beau,' she assured him tightly. 'I'm the one that kissed you—remember?'

He grimaced. 'Only after I had made it obvious that's what I intended doing to you if you invited me inside!'

Jaz shrugged. 'Then it's probably as well that we remained outside and discovered just how dangerous that would have been!'

Beau gave a rueful shake of his head. 'You really are an amazing young lady, Jaz.'

And perhaps that was part of the problem—she was young. She was also inexperienced. And obviously vulnerable. Not a good combination for a sophisticated man like Beau to become involved in!

'Thanks!' she accepted dryly. 'I'm also tired—so if you'll excuse me…?' she added pointedly.

'Of course.' He stepped back abruptly, hand still thrust into his pockets. 'And I meant what I said earlier. About your not having to get in to work too early in the morning,' he explained at her questioning look.

'Oh that.' She nodded understandingly, relieved it was something as innocuous as that. 'But if you're already thinking of moving on…' her voice had deepened huskily just at the thought of Beau leaving Aberton 'perhaps you would rather I didn't continue with the work I've started? No point in paying out all that money if you aren't going to be staying,' she added reluctantly.

She had already spent a substantial amount of that money on stocking up her freezer and buying a few other necessities—like new shoes and underwear! If she now had to return it…! Somehow she doubted Beau would be interested in frozen ready-to-eat meals, or the size four shoes, and as for the underwear—!

'No, just leave things as they are for the moment,' Beau reassured her by answering. 'Now you really should get inside—you're starting to turn blue!'

She felt as if she were too, the temperature having dropped dramatically this evening, freezing everything, including the snow that had fallen over the weekend.

'Take care,' she said abruptly in parting as she turned to go into the house—relieved when Beau didn't remark that she sounded like his mother again.

What a disastrous evening, she sighed as she closed

the door behind her. The beautiful Camilla fawning over Beau all through dinner. Her teeth-gnashing jealousy. Kissing Beau in that forward way. Realizing that she was in love with him!

In fact, the only positive thing that had happened this evening was that there wasn't another anonymous letter waiting for her on the doormat when she came in.

CHAPTER TWELVE

THERE had been no letter last night. But that fact had been rectified by the next morning when Jaz came wearily down the stairs at seven-thirty to make herself a cup of coffee.

She hadn't slept well, tossing and turning as she re-lived the embarrassment she had caused both Beau and herself the evening before by kissing him in the way that she had. Coming down the stairs to see yet another familiar white envelope laying on the mat in front of the door was not conducive to improving her mood.

The single word written there didn't help. 'Bitch!' it read simply.

Wonderful. Just what she wanted to hear. Just what she needed to pick herself up on this bright and frosty morning.

Didn't this person ever sleep? Creeping around either in the dead of night, or maybe very early this morning, in order to deliver this letter in time for her to see as soon as she got up.

Jaz gave a shiver just at the thought of this as-yet-faceless person being anywhere near her cottage. What sort of person did this? What sort of human being de-liberately taunted and hurt another one?

Not anyone that she wanted to know, Jaz decided as she ripped the letter and envelope in half as she strode into the kitchen, dropping them into the bin in passing.

It didn't take two guesses as to what she was being called a bitch for; this person was obviously aware she had been to Madelaine's the previous evening in Beau's company.

Well, that probably covered half the village by now! After all, the milkman had already been round on his delivery, and Betty Booth, always an early riser, might have stopped to have a chat with him about her meal out the previous evening, which he would then pass on to any other customers who happened to be up to take their delivery.

It was as simple as that, Jaz knew from experience. Not that it helped her in trying to discover who it was who was sending the letters, but it was somehow comforting to hope that it might be someone she didn't particularly like, either.

There was even the driver of the car with the intrusive headlights to consider. Maybe it had been a coincidence that they had driven by at that particular time, but, then again, maybe it hadn't.

Jaz frowned as she rebuked herself for not taking more notice of the make of car at least, its colour pretty indistinguishable in the darkness. But, then, she had been more preoccupied with Beau at the time than taking notice of an intrusive car!

And she was definitely becoming paranoid, she decided firmly. She didn't want to get to the stage where she took notice of passing cars, random or otherwise, to look with suspicion on anyone and everyone she spoke to, to guard her words on the off chance she could be talking to the 'wrong' person. Down that particular road lay—

She almost dropped the mug of coffee she had just made as the telephone rang shrilly in the hallway, her heart still racing even as she recognized it for the innocuous ringing of an incoming telephone call. Maybe it was already too late to tell herself not to become paranoid!

But, then, who could possibly be telephoning her at seven-forty in the morning, anyway? Maybe this anonymous tormentor had got tired of just sending letters and decided to telephone her to add weight to the accusations?

Only one way to find out, Jaz, she told herself firmly as she gritted her teeth and picked up the receiver. 'Yes?' she prompted abruptly.

'And a good morning to you too, Jaz Logan,' Beau's unmistakable voice came back teasingly. 'Had a bad night?' he added sympathetically.

And a bad morning too so far, she acknowledged, tearful with relief just at the sound of Beau's voice. Which really wouldn't do at all.

'Not really. What can I do for you?' she added briskly.

There was a brief silence at the other end of the line, as if Beau were debating what he should say in answer to that. 'The ground is frozen,' he finally answered her crisply. 'The temperature isn't forecast to change much, so I don't really think there's any point in your coming over to work today.'

Jaz felt her heart sink at this. Not that it wouldn't have been slightly embarrassing seeing Beau again after the way they had parted yet again last night, but, having received yet another of those unsettling letters, just being somewhere near Beau would have felt somehow reassuring. Being told there was no point in her going over definitely took her mood back down to despondent.

What was she going to do all day? Catch up on her bills, tend the plants with old Fred, everything that she used to before Beau Garrett came to the village, came the unequivocal answer.

Yes, but she didn't want to do any of those things today. What she wanted—

'There's no point in your coming over to work,' Beau repeated lightly, 'but I'll make you some lunch if you want to come over about twelve-thirty.'

Jaz frowned, totally stunned. 'You'll make me lunch?' she repeated slowly.

'Do you think that I can't?' Beau said dryly.

'No, it isn't that. I just—you—'

'I'm running hot and cold,' he provided with a sigh. 'Or, in this case, hot, cold, and then hot again.'

'Something like that,' she agreed.

'In my own defence, I would like to reassure you that this inconsistency of mood is not normal for me,' he came back self-derisively. 'I just—you have me confused, Jaz Logan.'

Her eyes widened. 'I do?'

'You do,' he sighed again. 'Again, not an emotion I'm used to. I have—had,' he corrected dryly, 'a well-ordered life. For obvious reasons I decided to make some changes in that life. But those changes did not include meeting someone like you.'

Jaz couldn't even pretend to know what he was talking about, the only thing really registering with her being the fact that Beau was inviting her over for lunch today. 'I would love to come over for lunch,' she told him lightly, at the same time sticking her tongue out at the bin where that third damning letter had been so recently disposed of. Bah sucks, she mentally added for good measure. Which probably made her as childish as the person who had been sending those ridiculous letters!

But she didn't care. She was not about to have some faceless person dictate to her where she should go and whom she should see.

'Someone like me?' she repeated lightly.

'Stop fishing, Jaz,' Beau told her mockingly. 'I've already said enough on that subject for one day,' he added disgustedly. 'Besides, isn't it enough that, against my better judgement, I'm inviting you over for lunch?'

'How graciously put, Mr Garrett!' she taunted—if only to hide how inwardly thrilled she was at the thought of seeing Beau again later today. Even if it was 'against his better judgement'... Quite what he meant by that, she wasn't sure, but it sounded promising.

'No one has ever accused me of being that—thank goodness!' he came back derisively. 'Now are you coming to lunch or aren't you?'

She was. She most definitely was. Even if she didn't have a clue what his 'better judgement' was telling him he should do!

'I am,' she confirmed lightly. 'Do you want me to bring anything with me?'

'Just yourself,' Beau answered gruffly.

Jaz felt that now familiar frisson of excitement down the length of her spine, a sense of some sort of inner warmth that she couldn't quite explain, but felt anyway.

'In that case, I'll see you at twelve-thirty,' she said huskily before ringing off.

She continued to stand in the hallway for some time after ending the call, lost in happy reverie at the thought of being with Beau again so soon, wondering what she could wear that wouldn't be over the top for a lunch, but at the same time was a step up from the scruffy denims and baggy jumpers Beau usually saw her in.

Only to come crashing down again with a bump as

she remembered his uncertainty last night about staying on in Aberton. What would she do, loving him as she did, if he should decide to cut his losses and go back to London?

Well, that was a definite dampener, Jaz, she mentally rebuked herself; a real downer.

Although it didn't change the fact that the possibility may have to be faced. And sooner rather than later if Beau's disenchantment with village life was anything to go by.

Oh, well, she sighed, her feet firmly back on the ground as she trudged her way back up the stairs; she would have to cross that particular bridge when she came to it.

'I thought we would eat in the kitchen, if that's all right with you?' Beau told her as he preceded her down the hallway after opening the front door to her ring. 'As well as being the warmest room in the house, it's still also the only one that's really habitable,' he added ruefully.

She was only too happy to stay in the kitchen, had forgotten, until she actually parked the van outside and contemplated coming inside, just how depressing she found the idea of being inside this house, and the memories it evoked; the kitchen was the one room that looked nothing at all as it used to.

Until she got here she hadn't really given where she was going any actual thought, had just been pleased to be seeing Beau. But as she climbed out of the van she had felt that old sense of foreboding that had possessed her whenever she'd visited her grandparents here.

'What is it?' Beau prompted sharply.

Jaz forced a smile to her lips, shaking her head. 'Nothing,' she dismissed. 'And the kitchen is fine.'

Beau continued to look at her with narrowed eyes. 'This wasn't a happy house, was it,' he sighed.

Her eyes widened. 'What do you mean?'

He shrugged. 'The swing in the garden. The children's wallpaper in one of the bedrooms. It's all an illusion, isn't it,' he said grimly. 'It wasn't a happy house, was it,' he repeated hardly.

Jaz swallowed hard, her hands pushed into the back pockets of the new pair of denims she was wearing. 'No,' she confirmed huskily. 'I—you have to understand. My grandparents did the best they could, but they—' She broke off, not sure what else to say.

'They failed miserably,' Beau finished disgustedly. 'With your mother. And then with you.'

She gave a pained frown. 'You're being unkind, Beau. They were good people—'

'Were they?' He was suddenly standing much too close.

Overwhelmingly so, Jaz decided as she took a step backwards. 'Yes, they were,' she repeated firmly. 'But they were both already in their forties when my mother was born, had no real idea how to bring up a child of their own. And my mother—' She shook her head. 'I may as well tell you this, because someone else is sure to,' she acknowledged disgustedly.

'Why are they?' he rasped harshly.

'Because it's what people do—'

'Not the people I know,' he assured her hardly.

She sighed. 'Well it's different here!'

'You're not wrong about that,' Beau confirmed heavily.

Jaz looked at him through a haze of tears. 'Did you invite me here to lunch just so that you could upset me?'

'Far from it,' he assured her grimly. 'But that's what I seem to be doing anyway—isn't it?' he realized self-disgustedly.

'I'm afraid you'll have to get in line.' Jaz sighed wearily, knowing this lunch date wasn't turning out at all as she had wanted it to. If only it had been anywhere but here…!

Beau became suddenly still, his gaze searching. 'What's that supposed to mean?' he prompted slowly, alerting Jaz to the fact that she had said too much.

Far to much, to a man as astute as Beau. She was still reeling slightly from receiving that third letter of course, may have ripped it up and thrown it away, but could still see that one accusing word whenever she closed her eyes, could still feel the hurt those letters evoked.

'Nothing,' she dismissed briskly. 'You're right, Beau; it's this house. It—' She made a dismissive gesture with her hands. 'I'm just being silly,' she told him self-derisively. 'What are we having for lunch?' she prompted brightly.

'Well, I ought to be eating humble pie after the way I've just thoroughly upset you,' Beau acknowledged ruefully. 'I just—there should be someone looking after you, Jaz.' He gave an impatient shake of his head at the fact that there obviously wasn't.

She eyed him mockingly. 'Isn't that rather a chauvinistic thing to say in this day and age?'

'I said "looking after you", Jaz,' he said dryly. 'Not patronizing you!'

She gave a teasing smile, relieved to have the subject changed from that of her mother and grandparents.

'Some feminists might consider that to be the same thing!'

'Then they would be wrong,' he stated flatly. 'I'm my own person, but I wouldn't mind having someone looking after me. Someone who cared, that is.'

'Wouldn't you?' she prompted huskily, very much afraid that they were now onto even shakier ground than they had been a few minutes ago.

Beau seemed to be aware of it too, their gazes locked, the air charged with the sudden tension between them—

A tension that was abruptly broken as a bell rang intrusively.

'The timer on the oven,' Beau grimaced in realization, turning away to open the oven door. 'Damn it!' he muttered as he instantly burnt his hand on the handle.

'I think you could be right about needing someone to take care of you,' Jaz murmured as she moved to pick up the oven cloth and check the food in the oven.

'The packet said they needed to cook for forty-five minutes,' Beau spoke from behind her.

'They' being lasagnes, a lovely aroma filling the air as Jaz moved the baking tray to look at them. 'The packet appears to be correct,' she told him teasingly as she pulled the tray out of the oven and put it on top of the cooker.

'There's a salad in the fridge, and baked potatoes in the bottom of the oven,' Beau told her challengingly.

She smiled at his defensive tone. 'I was referring to a housekeeper just now when I said you needed someone to look after you,' she told him teasingly. 'I'm surprised you don't have one,' she added curiously.

Surely when he'd lived in London he hadn't looked after himself all the time? He must have led a very busy

life, would have had little time for things like shopping,
let alone cooking his own food.

'I hate having strangers in my home,' Beau answered
firmly. 'My ex-wife, then my wife, insisted that a man
in my position had to have a housekeeper, that I
couldn't possibly expect her to do the cooking and
housework, and so she brought her own housekeeper
with her when we got married,' he explained as Jaz
raised questioning brows. 'The last bit I can understand—maybe, but I never did work out what "a man
in my position" was exactly.' He grimaced.

Then he was the only one that hadn't, Jaz acknowledged ruefully.

'But it was like being a visitor in my own home,'
Beau continued disgustedly. 'Veronica and the housekeeper worked out the menus between them, and con-
sequently I was often served food I didn't want to eat.
I wasn't even allowed to relax on my own furniture, in
case I "made a mess"; I never quite worked that one
out either! I did know that I felt like a stranger in my
own home. I made sure that when Veronica left me the
housekeeper followed her out the door!' He gave a
scathing shake of his head.

He made his marriage sound like a battleground!
'Were you together for very long?' Jaz asked casually.

'Ten months, three days, and six hours!' Beau came
back grimly.

Definitely a battleground if he had the timing pinned
down so accurately!

Jaz had to hold back a smile at his vehemence. 'It
doesn't sound like much fun,' she said noncommittally.

'About as much fun as a trip to the dentist!' he acknowledged disgustedly. 'Which is why I decided I was

never going to put myself in that position ever again,' he added frowningly.

And he obviously hadn't. Although Jaz had a feeling this last comment was as much a warning to her as it was a statement of fact...

'After what you've just said, I can't say that I blame you,' she said brightly, determined not to show how affected she was by the comment.

Not that she had ever, in her wildest dreams, considered that Beau would ever consider marrying someone like her. But to hear him state his aversion to marriage in such blunt terms was a little disheartening, to say the least.

'No,' he confirmed broodingly, before turning away to busy himself taking the warm plates out of the oven and begin serving the food onto them.

Jaz stood ineffectually to one side, unsure what to do; the table was laid, the food was obviously ready to eat, and she—

The telephone began to ring on the wall, Jaz turning enquiringly to Beau as he swore under his breath at the noisy intrusion, the reason for his irritation becoming obvious as she saw he was in the middle of serving up the lasagne.

'Get that for me, will you, please?' he prompted impatiently.

Jaz frowned, not sure that having her answer Beau's telephone was a good idea; what if it were one of his friends from London, maybe a particular friend, how was she supposed to explain her presence here in his home...?

'Jaz!' Beau frowned across at her pointedly as the telephone continued to ring.

She gave a shrug before moving to pick up the receiver; if Beau didn't mind her answering his call, then why should she?

'Yes?' she prompted lightly into the receiver.

Silence.

'Hello?' Jaz enquired encouragingly.

Again silence.

Jaz felt a shiver of apprehension run the length of her spine, knew that there was someone on the other end of the telephone line, could hear them breathing; whoever it was just didn't want to speak to her!

'Hello?' she repeated more firmly, not in the least surprised when she heard the gentle click of the receiver being replaced at the other end of the line.

'Who is it?' Beau glanced across impatiently.

She swallowed hard. 'No one now,' she dismissed, her hand shaking as she replaced the receiver on the wall bracket. 'I guess they must have had a wrong number,' she added with a brightness she was far from feeling.

Because she didn't believe for a moment that the caller had got the wrong number; it had simply been the wrong person who had answered the call.

Because she was utterly convinced that whoever the person was who was sending her those anonymous letters, it was someone who knew Beau well enough to feel comfortable telephoning him, was convinced she had just spoken to the person who was sending her those letters.

CHAPTER THIRTEEN

'SIT down!' Beau instructed firmly. 'Put your head between your knees,' he added grimly once Jaz had sat down on one of the kitchen chairs.

It was either sit down or fall down!

Reaction had set in almost immediately Jaz realized she had actually been talking to her tormenter, the colour draining from her face, her legs beginning to shake. Beau had taken one look at her before dropping the tray containing the lasagne onto the draining-board and rushing over to her.

He came down on his haunches beside the chair, looking at her with concern as she began to straighten from her bent position; these jeans were still new enough not to be too comfortable for bending in!

'What is it?' Beau demanded sharply.

She shook her head. 'I—it was—'

'It was the telephone call,' he rasped shrewdly. 'I thought you said the call was a wrong number?' he prompted abruptly.

She swallowed hard, her mouth feeling very dry. 'It was,' she confirmed huskily.

His frown deepened. 'Then why have you gone the colour of wallpaper paste?'

She gave a humourless smile. 'Are you always this complimentary?'

'I'm usually even less effusive,' he assured her dryly. 'You must just bring out the best in me!'

He was attempting to make her laugh, and, despite

her inner misery, he succeeded, her smile genuine this time, if a little shaky. 'I'm sorry. I don't know what happened. One minute I was fine, the next—'

'It was the telephone call,' Beau repeated grimly. 'Who was it? Did they say something unpleasant to you?' His eyes narrowed questioningly.

Not a word. Not one word. But, then, they hadn't needed to...

'I told you, it was a wrong number,' she dismissed, turning away, her attention caught—thankfully!—by the tray of lasagne. 'Our lunch is getting cold,' she reminded lightly.

'Damn the lunch,' Beau bit out harshly. 'Jaz, you almost fainted just now, and if you think I'm just going to calmly carry on eating our lunch without first being given some sort of explanation for it, then you're sadly mistaken!'

'That's a pity; it's probably because I'm hungry that I almost fainted,' she said brightly, really not sure she would be able to eat when she still felt so sick, but determined not to give Beau the truthful explanation for her behaviour.

Because it wouldn't stop there. Beau would then demand to know everything that had happened the last couple of weeks. And goodness knew what he would do when he realized someone had been sending those horrible letters to her. And that her friendship with him was the reason for it...!

'Jaz...?' He gave her a warning look.

She opened innocently wide eyes. 'Beau?'

He sighed his frustration with her silence. 'There's something you aren't telling me,' he said slowly.

'A woman of mystery, that's me,' she agreed self-derisively.

His mouth tightened. 'Jaz—'

'I really am hungry, Beau.' She gave him a rueful smile.

He continued to look at her for several tense seconds, and then he gave an impatient sigh before straightening. 'Okay, I'm going to feed you,' he conceded. 'But then I'm going to demand an explanation rather than ask for one!'

She knew him well enough to believe him, but the time lapse might give her a chance to try and think of some sort of explanation for her near faint that he would accept. Not the truth, of course—

'A truthful one,' he added grimly—as if he had just read her thoughts!

Which he probably had, Jaz inwardly acknowledged; she wasn't too good at hiding her feelings!

But she did try very hard to do just that over the next half an hour or so, giving every impression of enjoying her meal as Beau continued to watch her closely—even though she had a feeling she was going to be extremely ill once she got away from here!

'Okay, that's it,' he finally announced impatiently, standing up to remove both their plates from the table, neither of them having done justice to the food on them. 'Explanation time,' he told Jaz grimly as he turned back to face her, his expression unmistakably uncompromising.

She drew in a deep breath. 'But we haven't finished our lunch,' she delayed.

His mouth twisted humourlessly. 'Probably because neither of us is enjoying it! Stop prevaricating, Jaz,' he added determinedly as she would have spoken again. 'I want to know what's going on,' he told her softly, his tone gentle.

It was that gentleness that was her undoing, her vision suddenly blurred by tears, tears that fell hotly down her cheeks before she could do anything to check them.

'Jaz...!' Beau groaned.

She heard him move across the room, felt herself pulled up to be cradled protectively in his arms. Which only made her cry all the harder!

She rested her cheek against his shirt-front, her arms about his waist as she leant into him, knowing she had only been delaying this reaction, that the silence earlier on the other end of that telephone call still haunted her.

Finally the tears slowed, and then stopped, and Jaz found herself held tightly in Beau's arms, one of his hands lightly smoothing her hair from temple to nape as he murmured to her soothingly.

She didn't move, relishing this time in his arms, knowing that when it stopped he would once again demand an explanation. One she was no further forward towards giving him than she had been an hour ago!

'Okay, Jaz,' he finally murmured dryly. 'I know you've stopped crying because I can almost hear the cogs of your brain ticking over as you try to think of some explanation that I will find acceptable!'

She raised her head to frown at him. 'I really don't have to explain anything to you, acceptable or not.'

He nodded. 'You really do,' he assured her mildly.

'No—'

'Yes, Jaz, you really do.' He enunciated clearly and firmly, holding her at arm's length to hold her gaze unblinkingly.

Jaz frowned her frustration with his determination. There was always the possibility that she had made a mistake, that it was just because of her earlier tension about receiving that third anonymous letter that had made her jump to the conclusion that Beau's telephone call wasn't a wrong number. Which would make telling Beau about those letters completely unnecessary.

None of which, she could see by Beau's grimly determined expression, he would be willing to accept...

She gave a dismissive shrug. 'I thought perhaps the call was from—from a woman, someone who found it rather odd that another woman should be answering your telephone, and that was the reason they hung up.'

Beau's gaze narrowed. 'And if it was? Why should that upset you?'

Yes, why should it? Unless she was in love with him herself. Which, of course, she was, but she didn't want Beau to know that!

She swallowed hard. 'I—you've been so kind to me, I—I wouldn't want to cause any problems between you and—and—'

'A woman who hangs up when another woman answers my telephone,' Beau finished dryly.

'Exactly!' she agreed gratefully.

He gave a decisive shake of his head. 'I don't know any women who would do that.'

Her eyes widened. 'You don't?'

'No,' he assured her positively.

Did that mean that there wasn't a woman in his life who might do that? Or did it mean that the woman currently in his life, as far as he was concerned, didn't have the right to do that?

The trouble was, she was so inexperienced in these things, had no idea how a man like Beau might conduct his private life.

'Oh,' she grimaced awkwardly. 'In that case—'

'It wasn't anyone I know—or want to know!—who

ended the call in that abrupt way.' His gaze was narrowed shrewdly. 'So who do you think it was, Jaz?'

She had a feeling she knew what it was, if not exactly who. But she was still loath to discuss those anonymous letters with Beau. Although, she accepted that after today, she would have to discuss them with someone.

She made a dismissive gesture. 'It's your telephone, Beau,' she reminded him wryly.

His hands dropped down from her arms as he stepped away from her. 'So it is,' he accepted lightly. 'Okay, Jaz, let's try approaching this from a different angle; you were going to tell me something about your mother when you first arrived...?'

Reminding her that the investigative reporter in this man was far from retired!

She managed a dismissive laugh. 'You're being a little unfair now, Beau,' she rebuked ruefully. 'Besides—' she glanced at her wrist-watch '—it's time I was going.' She collected her jacket. 'I can't leave poor old Fred alone at the garden centre all day.'

Beau crossed his arms over his chest as he looked at her. 'This prick of conscience concerning poor old Fred is a little late in coming, isn't it?' he drawled.

'I had two customers this morning, I'll have you know,' she told him primly.

'Wow,' he mocked.

Yes, wow. One of them had wanted a dozen bedding plants, and the other two bags of fertilizer, not exactly the thing successful businesses were made of. Which was why she was giving leaving Aberton some serious thought...

She shrugged. 'It's a start,' she dismissed. 'Thank you for lunch, Beau, it was—'

'A dismal failure,' he finished harshly.

She raised dark brows. 'In what way?'

Despite her emotional wobble earlier she had recovered—just. Lunch had been more than edible—in fact she was sorry she couldn't have done it more justice. Their conversation as they ate had been pleasantly impersonal. And, once again, just now she had fended off his interest in her earlier emotional wobble, so in what way did he think it had been a failure?

He gave a shake of his head. 'You don't want to know,' he rasped.

Jaz frowned now. 'But I do. I admit that I was a little silly earlier, but—'

'Jaz, you did not do anything wrong, all right?' Once again his hands tightly gripped her upper arms, painfully so as he shook her slightly. 'In fact,' he bit out between gritted teeth, 'hard as I try, there isn't a damn thing I can find to dislike about you!'

Her frown turned to bewilderment. 'You want to find something to dislike about me...?'

His face was pale, a nerve pulsing in his tightly clenched jaw. 'Yes, I want to find something to dislike about you!' he snapped. 'Maybe you talk in your sleep? Snore?' he added as she gave a negative shake of her head. 'Not that either of those things is too important in the grand scheme of things,' he added disgustedly as Jaz gave another puzzled shake of her head. 'But there has to be something—'

'My inferiority complex "the size of a house"?' she put in helpfully.

Beau gave a shout of laughter, shaking his head as he sobered. 'Jaz, you aren't supposed to help me in this!'

'Sorry!' She grimaced.

His laughter turned to a chuckle, his gaze warmly affectionate as he looked down at her. 'You see,' he gave a rueful shake of his head. 'Even when I'm being less than kind to you, instead of being angry, you turn around and make me laugh! What am I supposed to do with you?' he muttered self-disgustedly.

Jaz swallowed hard as she looked up at him, aware that the atmosphere had suddenly changed between them, now charged with—she wasn't sure what it was charged with! She did know that Beau's hands had stopped painfully gripping her arms and were now lightly caressing, that his impatient anger of a few minutes ago had turned into something she couldn't quite define—but it was definitely no longer anger.

She moistened dry lips. 'What do you want to do with me?' she prompted huskily.

He gave an impatient shake of his head. 'Jaz, what I really want to do to you would frighten the hell out of you!'

'No—'

'Yes!' he insisted harshly. 'And therein lies my problem.' He sighed deeply. 'With any other woman it would be a simple matter of satisfying the curiosity and moving on.'

Her throat felt dry, her voice coming out as a rasp. 'But not with me?'

'No, not with you.' He sighed again. 'Jaz, you're twenty-five, and I shall be forty in two months' time—'

'Which means you're only thirty-nine now,' she cut in pointedly, her pulse racing.

'Pedantic,' he muttered.

'Not at all,' she assured him softly. 'You see, in two months' time, I shall be twenty-six.'

He blinked. 'The tenth of May.'

'*I'm* the tenth of May.' She nodded, her eyes glowing with laughter at his less-than-pleased expression at the fact that they had the same birthday.

Beau shook his head. 'This is too much!'

'What is?'

'All of this!' He moved away impatiently. 'I moved to Aberton because I was tired of London, of the people, of the life I lived there—and within days of moving here I literally bump into you!' He gave another impatient shake of his head. 'Someone up there—' he glanced skywards '—has it in for me!'

Jaz shrugged. 'In that case, isn't it more likely to be "someone down there"?' She glanced towards the floor.

He looked stunned for a moment, and then he gave a rueful smile. 'It could be—but taking into account the fact that it's you, somehow I doubt it! Jaz—'

'Beau,' she interrupted firmly, taking a step towards him, still not completely sure of all the implications of this conversation, but sure enough to realize that Beau liked her. Unless she was mistaken, a lot more than he wanted to...!

He glanced at her warily as she stood only inches away from him. 'What?' He tried to sound aggressive, but the fact that he was so disturbed by her closeness completely negated the effort.

Jaz smiled shyly. 'I like you too,' she told him huskily.

He groaned, closing his eyes briefly, those eyes glittering silver when he opened them again. 'Jaz, you can't just go around telling men you like them—'

'Why can't I?'

'Because that isn't the way it's done!' he said impatiently.

'But I just did tell you I like you,' she pointed out reasoningly.

'I know you did,' he acknowledged impatiently. 'But I—you—Jaz, you're just a baby compared to me! I've been married, for goodness' sake, and I wasn't a saint before or after that marriage, either, whereas you—' He broke off, breathing hard in his frustration with this situation.

'"Whereas I"…?' she prompted softly.

He blinked, his expression softening as he looked at her. 'You're all brand-new, Jaz. Untouched. All youth and vitality, and as yet unfulfilled dreams—'

'You don't sound as if your dreams have been fulfilled yet, either,' she cut in softly, her heart beating a tattoo in her chest, barely breathing in the tension of the moment.

He gave a humourless smile. 'Maybe my dreams were never the same as yours!'

She looked at him closely, at those guarded grey eyes, the cynicism of his expression, the wary stance of his body. 'Oh, I think that they were,' she finally said slowly. 'I just think they got slightly bruised along the way.'

'You see!' he bit out tensely. 'There's no reasoning with you!'

Her lips curved into a smile. 'Only because you know I'm right.'

He gave a derisive smile. 'Since when did you become so wise, Jaz Logan?'

She wasn't in the least daunted by his taunting tone. 'A person's age doesn't necessarily make them wise or unwise, it's the life they've lived that does that,' she said quietly.

Beau's look became searching. 'And the life you

lived with your parents and grandparents has given you a wisdom beyond your years,' he guessed huskily.

'Yes,' she confirmed simply.

She didn't have the experience, or the worldliness, that Beau was probably used to in the people he spent time with, but her knowledge of people was no less than his own.

'Jaz…!' Beau reached out and took her into his arms, at the same time his mouth coming down possessively on hers.

All of today, probably all of yesterday evening, too, had been building up to this moment, the attraction between them so strong it was impossible to deny, Jaz's lips opening to deepen the kiss, her arms up about his shoulders, her fingers enmeshed in the dark thickness of his hair.

She loved this man. Was in love with him, too. Wanted nothing more than to spend the rest of her life with him.

But if that wasn't to be, then she wanted now with him!

He felt so good, his skin firm as she unbuttoned his shirt, covered in fine dark hair, tiny goose bumps of pleasure appearing as she broke their kiss, her lips following the same path as her hands, Beau groaning low in his throat as her tongue flicked lightly over his sensitivity.

She was guided completely by instinct, only knew that she wanted to touch Beau and be touched by him, wanted to completely lose herself in him, wanted—

There was a sudden clattering noise overhead, a loud curse, the sound of something sliding, and then that something crashing to the ground outside the kitchen window.

CHAPTER FOURTEEN

'WHAT the—?' Beau blinked dazedly.

Jaz was as stunned as Beau by this unexpected interruption, but they realized in unison the possible source of the noise.

'Dennis!' Jaz cried concernedly.

'Davis!' Beau rasped grimly.

They both rushed across to the kitchen door, hurrying outside to stand on the pathway and look up at the roof.

Dennis Davis stood poised on the rooftop, a sheepish expression on his face as he looked down at them. 'Sorry about that. One of the roof slates slipped out of my hand.'

Now that they were outside, Jaz could see that was the case, found herself actually standing on some of the smashed slate.

Well, on the positive side, at least Dennis hadn't actually fallen off the roof himself, as they had at first suspected. But on the negative side, what on earth was Dennis doing letting slates slide off the roof in that dangerous way; it was pure luck that no one had been actually standing on this pathway when the slate had dropped!

From the look on Beau's face, now that his initial concern had been satisfied, it was the latter side that interested him!

'Get off my roof,' he growled at the other man.

Dennis looked stunned. 'But—'

'Now,' Beau grated coldly.

Jaz touched his arm. 'I'm sure it was only an accident, Beau,' she said soothingly.

'An accident that should never have happened,' he snapped without taking his gaze off the older man as he carefully manoeuvred his way down from the roof. 'Now get off my property,' he told the other man as he stepped down onto the path beside him.

Dennis still looked dazed. 'But I've only half finished the job.' He frowned.

'Half started it, you mean,' Beau rasped scathingly. 'Take yourself, and any of the equipment that happens to be yours, and go. And don't bother to come back,' he added grimly.

Dennis turned to Jaz. 'It was just a little accident,' he began wheedlingly.

'A costly one—for you,' Beau was the one to answer him before Jaz could even think of a suitable reply.

Actually, she thought he was probably being a little harsh on the older man; Dennis never had been known for his efficiency. Beau had no idea how lucky he was that Dennis had continued to turn up to do the job at all!

'Did I disturb you in the middle of something?' Dennis eyed the younger man speculatively.

'Go,' Beau told the other man with barely controlled violence, his hands clenched into fists at his sides.

Dennis took one more look at the younger man's face, shot Jaz a raised-brow look, and went.

Jaz looked at Beau too now, realizing the reason for Dennis's last comment as she saw that Beau's shirt was still unbuttoned from their lovemaking earlier, his tanned skin covered in fine dark hair. Skin and hair she had caressed and kissed only minutes earlier...

Colour darkened her cheeks as she accepted that little

gem of information would quickly pass around the village, no doubt greatly embellished now that Dennis had actually been sacked from working here any longer!

Beau frowned across at her. 'What is it?'

She shook her head. 'I'm just not sure that sacking Dennis in that way was a good idea.'

Beau's expression darkened. 'The man is completely incompetent. What if you had been standing under here at the time?' he added grimly. 'Damn it, you could have been killed!'

'So could you,' she pointed out huskily, finding the very idea of that made her feel sick.

Beau took a step towards her. 'Jaz—'

'Hello, you two,' greeted a warm friendly voice that Jaz instantly recognized as Madelaine.

'Your shirt, Beau!' she managed to mutter before turning to smile at the older woman, effectively blocking Madelaine's view of Beau as she did so, giving him time to button up his shirt; no point in adding to the speculation by piquing Madelaine's curiosity concerning his partly undressed state!

Madelaine looked as beautiful as ever today in a deep red trouser suit and white silk blouse, showing no adverse effects of having had guests staying with her over the weekend.

'I've just passed a very disgruntled-looking Dennis Davis in the driveway,' she told them ruefully after kissing them both on the cheek in greeting.

'I sacked him for incompetence,' Beau stated flatly, moving to stand at Jaz's side, his shirt neatly rebuttoned.

'Oh, dear,' Madelaine sympathized. 'I did try to warn you that the man is a terrible slacker.'

'An idiot would be a more apt description,' Beau rasped disgustedly.

Madelaine shot Jaz a questioning grimace. A question Jaz wasn't completely sure how to answer. Yes, Dennis was less than efficient at what he did—but, in his favour, no one had ever claimed otherwise, least of all him! And to be honest, she was still slightly stunned herself with the way Beau had just sacked the other man on the spot...

'He certainly isn't worth forgetting my manners!' Beau sighed impatiently. 'Come inside, Madelaine, and join us for a cup of coffee.'

'Lovely,' the other woman accepted warmly. 'I've just driven the last of my guests to the railway station and wished them a happy journey,' she explained lightly as they all went into the kitchen. 'I was just driving past when I saw Jaz's van outside and thought I would pop in and say hello to you both,' she added brightly.

Jaz was still feeling slightly uncomfortable from Beau's remark of 'join us' for a cup of coffee; almost as if the two of them were a couple, instead of host and guest. Madelaine's comment about popping in to say hello to 'you both' only seemed to add to that air of intimacy...!

'You were lucky you didn't arrive a few minutes earlier,' Beau told the other woman disgustedly as he prepared the coffee percolator. 'You could have had a roof slate crash down on your head if you had,' he explained grimly.

'Oh, dear, is that what Dennis did?' Madelaine grimaced. 'I say, I haven't interrupted your lunch, have I?' she exclaimed as she saw the remains of their meal on the table.

'Not at all,' Jaz answered firmly, deftly picking up

the mats and condiments and placing them on a worktop out of the way. 'I was actually just about to leave...' she added pointedly, only to have Beau glance across at her frowningly.

Whether it was genuinely because he wanted her to stay and have coffee, or just that he didn't want to be left alone here with Madelaine, Jaz wasn't quite sure.

In either case, she took pity on him. 'But a coffee would be nice,' she accepted dryly. 'I was going to telephone you this afternoon anyway, Madelaine,' she told the other woman as the two of them sat down at the kitchen table. 'To thank you for a lovely evening yesterday,' she added lightly.

Madelaine beamed. 'It was rather fun, wasn't it.'

Fun wasn't quite how Jaz would have described the evening, but it certainly wasn't Madelaine's fault she hadn't enjoyed herself.

'Yes, thanks for a great evening,' Beau said as he placed the cups of coffee down on the table, along with the cream and sugar, before sitting down to join them. 'We'll have to return the favour,' he continued decisively. 'I take it you can cook, Jaz?' He raised mocking brows in her direction.

Jaz looked across at him frowningly. What on earth did he think he was he doing? They weren't a couple, there was no 'we', and, as such, it was totally irrelevant whether or not she could cook!

'More than my take-it-out-of-a-packet-and-stick-it-in-the-oven-lasagne, at any rate,' he added self-derisively.

She could cook, yes, had done so a lot when her father had still been alive, and they had been left on their own. Although she was sadly out of practise in recent years, tended to just get herself whatever was easiest.

'I'm sure you underestimate yourself, Beau.' Madelaine laughed appreciatively.

'No, I don't,' he assured her dryly. 'But if we can persuade Jaz into cooking the meal, perhaps you would like to come to dinner on Saturday evening?'

And 'perhaps' he should have asked 'Jaz' first whether or not she wanted to come here on Saturday evening and cook them all a meal!

Because then he would have learnt that the answer was no! Not that she thought the information about this initial invitation would go any further than Madelaine; the other woman certainly wasn't one of the village gossips. But if the dinner actually took place, it was sure to become public knowledge, whether they wanted it to or not. And Jaz certainly didn't want it to!

'I would love to,' Madelaine accepted graciously. 'Jaz?' she enquired teasingly.

Madelaine obviously found this as funny as Beau did, and in the circumstances Jaz couldn't exactly blame her. But her friend didn't know about those anonymous letters.

But to give him credit, neither did Beau...

'Fine.' She nodded abruptly—but with the intention of getting herself out of it as soon as she had a chance to talk to Beau alone. Which she was going to do before she left today!

However, that didn't happen for some time, the three of them chatting amiably as they drank their coffee, Madelaine the one to finally look at her watch and excuse herself.

'I have an appointment at the hairdresser's this afternoon,' she explained as she stood up. 'But I'll see you both on Saturday,' she added with a teasing look in Jaz's direction.

'We'll look forward to it,' Beau was the one to answer smoothly.

'You may be looking forward to it.' Jaz turned on him as soon as she heard Madelaine's car depart. 'I most certainly am not.' Her eyes flashed deeply blue. 'What do you mean by inviting Madelaine to dinner with us both?'

'Calm down,' Beau soothed as he cleared the cups from the table. 'I thought I was doing you a favour by having the dinner here, that's all.' He shrugged.

'Doing me a favour!' Jaz repeated incredulously.

'Well, you have to admit, this house is bigger than your cottage for entertaining,' he nodded unconcernedly.

'If I was intending to entertain—which I wasn't!' she snapped accusingly.

Beau shrugged. 'It just seemed to me that we both owed Madelaine a dinner.'

They probably did. In fact, the amount of times Jaz had either been to Madelaine's for afternoon tea, or a dinner, she probably owed the other woman a lot more than one dinner; she just wasn't happy with the idea of jointly entertaining with Beau, of all people.

'What's the problem, Jaz?' he prompted lightly. 'I'm sure between the two of us we can come up with something edible.'

'It isn't a question of that.' She shook her head impatiently.

For someone who had a very short time ago complained to the fates for even introducing the two of them, he had a very strange way of wanting to keep his distance!

'Then what is it a question of?' He tilted his head to one side as he looked at her questioningly.

The fact was, she was in love with this man, and it was going to be sheer torture coming here on Saturday and preparing dinner with him as if they really were a couple.

'I just don't think this is a good idea, that's all,' she muttered disgruntledly.

He shrugged. 'Madelaine didn't seem to find anything unusual about it.'

No, she hadn't—which only made it all the more obvious that people were starting to think of Jaz and Beau as a couple. A completely mismatched one! It was also going to make things more difficult for her when Beau decided to move on...

She glared at him. 'I think you might have consulted me first before making the invitation!'

'There was no opportunity to do that with Madelaine sitting there,' he pointed out derisively.

Jaz's mouth firmed. 'Even so...'

'Even so what?' Beau taunted, stepping forward until he stood only inches away from her. 'You know, Jaz, anyone would think it was me you didn't want to have dinner with on Saturday evening.' He arched mocking brows. 'Which certainly wasn't the impression I had before Davis inopportunely dropped that slate off the roof.' His mouth tightened at the memory.

She could feel the warmth in her cheeks at being reminded of the impression Beau had got of her before Dennis had had his accident; if Dennis hadn't interrupted them when he had then she had no doubts that Madelaine would have arrived at an even more inopportune moment!

Beau's hand moved to cup her cheek, his thumb moving to caress the softness of her lips. 'The next time we make love, Jaz, I would like it to be in the comfort of a bed, with a little privacy thrown in.'

The next time?

Was there going to be a next time?

The sensuous warmth in Beau's gaze seemed to say there was. But what of her? How would she feel about that if Beau left the village, as he kept threatening to do?

She stepped back, Beau's hand falling back to his side, his gaze narrowing guardedly. 'I don't think that's a good idea, Beau,' she told him evenly, her outer calm totally belied by the pounding of her heart in her chest.

She was in love with this man, wanted nothing more than to make love with him. But she still had no idea how he felt about her—other than the fact that he liked her and obviously wished that he didn't! Not a very good basis from which to start any sort of relationship.

'No?' he prompted tightly.

'No.' She gave a decisive shake of her head. 'But you are right about my owing Madelaine dinner,' she continued lightly, knowing she owed the other woman so much more than that for the times she had helped her just by listening the last few years. 'And The Old Vicarage is bigger than my cottage. It's just—'

'You're uncomfortable being the hostess here,' Beau completed abruptly. 'I should have thought of that,' he muttered self-disgustedly. 'Should have realized that this is the last place you would want to play hostess.' He shook his head grimly. 'I'll telephone Madelaine later and tell her there's been a change of venue.'

As far as Jaz was concerned, that really would be for the best, but somehow she thought Madelaine might be more comfortable here...

'No, leave things as they are.' She sighed her capitulation. 'I'll just have to get used to the idea, won't I?' Her smile was rueful as she looked at Beau. 'Now I really must be going; I still have quite a lot of work to do today.' And a need to put as much distance as possible between herself and Beau for the immediate future!

She needed time—and space—to sort out her own emotions. If they could be sorted out! Falling in love with Beau certainly complicated her life...

'If it helps, Jaz...' Beau spoke softly '...I'm just as unsettled by all of this as you are,' he admitted ruefully.

No, it didn't help. Because Beau had the determination—and the means—of putting anything he felt for her away in the deepest region of his heart, never to be looked at again, whereas she knew she couldn't do that!

She gave a humourless smile. 'It doesn't.'

He grimaced. 'I had a feeling it wouldn't. But at least I tried.' He shrugged.

She glanced across to where he had stacked the plates from lunch. 'Do you want me to help clear away?'

'No.'

'I—well, okay.' She nodded. 'Thank you for lunch. I—I'll be seeing you.'

'I would hazard a guess that you can count on it,' Beau confirmed dryly.

So would she. They were like two magnets, attracting and yet repelling at one and the same time.

The question was, which of those two forces was going to ultimately be the stronger?

CHAPTER FIFTEEN

'BUT, Jaz, who could possibly do such a thing?' Madelaine's shock showed clearly on her beautifully made-up face.

Jaz had arrived home from having lunch with Beau a couple of hours ago, only to find yet another letter waiting inside for her on the doormat. There were three words printed on the sheet of white paper this time, all the same word, but obviously written with increasing fury. 'Liar, liar, LIAR.'

She had been so stunned by this second letter arriving in one day that for some time she had just dropped down onto the stairs and sat there in a daze.

Shortly after that the tears had come. Painful, bewildered tears, running hotly and unchecked down her cheeks as she tried to make sense of the nightmare this had become.

But as the tears ceased, and the pain lessened, to become replaced by an anger that was just as forceful, she had known that the time for sitting here in silence was over, that she had to talk to someone about these horrible letters. Madelaine, her only ally over the last few years, had been the obvious choice, and, only waiting long enough to be sure the other woman had returned from the beauty salon, she had driven the short distance to see her.

'And you say there have been several others?' Madelaine prompted frowningly, still holding this latest letter in her hand, her freshly painted nails showing blood-red against the whiteness of the paper.

'Yes,' Jaz confirmed gruffly. 'At first, I—I thought it was just someone's idea of a joke—'

'No one could possibly believe this was in the least funny!' Madelaine snorted disgustedly, her fingers tightening on the letter she held. 'What have you done with the other letters?' she prompted frowningly.

'Thrown them in the bin,' Jaz admitted with a sigh.

'Not clever, Jaz, that just makes their existence your word against—whoever,' Madelaine rebuked gently.

Her eyes widened. 'No one could possibly believe I would make up a thing like this!'

'No,' the older woman acknowledged with distaste. 'Have you talked to Beau about them?' A frown marred the creaminess of her brow.

'Certainly not,' Jaz dismissed anxiously.

'I thought not,' Madelaine nodded slowly.

'And I don't want him to know, either,' Jaz insisted forcefully.

'Why on earth not?' Her friend frowned.

Jaz turned away slightly. 'Because—because—how would it look?' she prompted impatiently. 'He's already told me he's disenchanted with village life, if he knew about those letters he would leave here so fast none of us would see him for the dust!'

Madelaine shook her head slowly. 'I think you're underestimating him, Jaz. I'm sure he'd take charge... control the situation, even confront the sender.' She lingered persuasively over the words.

Maybe she was underestimating him, but she still didn't want Beau to know about those letters, knew that it was because of her friendship with him that the letters were being sent in the first place. He may just decide that the best way to stop them was for the two of them not to be friends any more!

'Jaz, you do realize you have to go to the police—'

'No, I don't.' She stood up agitatedly, snatching the letter back out of Madelaine's hand before crumpling it into a ball. 'I only—I just needed to tell someone about them, Madelaine. Promise me you won't tell anyone else.' She looked at the other woman beseechingly.

'But, Jaz—'

'Please, Madelaine!'

The older woman sighed. 'Okay, I promise. But only on condition that you promise me you will seriously think about informing the police,' she added firmly. 'It's horrible, Jaz,' she continued gently. 'And there's always the possibility it may not stop at just letters.'

She became suddenly still, her face pale as she looked down at Madelaine. 'What do you mean?'

The older woman shrugged. 'Think about it, Jaz. The letters are increasing, definitely becoming more vitriolic; the next step may be damage to either your property—or you.'

'But I just—I can't believe—' She gave a dazed shake of her head. 'Do you really think it might come to that?'

'Don't you?' Madelaine prompted gently.

Until this moment she hadn't really given the idea any thought. But the letters were becoming more frequent, and definitely angrier, so wasn't what Madelaine suggested a possible next step?

She swallowed hard. 'No,' she answered firmly. 'I think it's just someone being nasty because of—well, because of the way my mother behaved,' she concluded huskily. 'It's horrible. And painful. But no one could seriously believe, because of what happened, that I could do something like that too. Besides, Beau is no longer a married man,' she added determinedly. 'So why shouldn't I be friends with him?'

'Well, yes, but aren't you becoming more than friends?' Madelaine asked. 'Don't you think all this is because you're a couple?'

'We are not a couple!' Jaz snapped.

'Of course you aren't.' Madelaine's eyes gleamed. 'I say,' she added suddenly, 'you don't think Dennis Davis could have something to do with these letters, do you? Or that creepy sister of his that he lives with?' she added with a frown. 'Beau did sack Dennis earlier today, and Margaret Davis is a frustrated spinster if ever I've seen one.'

Jaz had been through all of this in her own mind in the hours since she received this latest letter, and, much as she found Margaret Davis as unpleasant as her brother, she didn't think the elderly lady was capable of doing something like this.

She gave a dismissive shake of her head. 'I doubt she even knows how to use a computer.'

'Oh, but she does,' Madelaine corrected, sitting forward avidly in her chair. 'She's the one who sends out all Dennis's bills for him.' She stood up to move to the bureau that stood in the corner of her little sitting room where she and Jaz had been drinking tea. 'Here.' She pulled out a letter, unfolding it to show Jaz the last bill she had received from 'Dennis Davis, Builder'.

It was printed on similar—identical—paper to that the letters had been written on. And it had been printed out on a computer...

Jaz gave a shake of her head. 'This doesn't prove anything—except that most households nowadays have, or have access to, computers,' she grimaced.

'I still think you should talk to the police—'

'No!' Jaz repeated firmly. 'The letters are just—unpleasant. They aren't threatening or anything like that.'

Madelaine still frowned worriedly. 'But—'

'No, Madelaine,' she cut in gently. 'I've talked to you about this; let's just leave it at that, hmm?' she prompted encouragingly.

She was really wishing now that she had never come to Madelaine and talked to her like this. The whole situation had been better when it was just herself that knew about the letters. And the person sending them...

Her mouth tightened as she thought of that faceless person, her earlier anger only just below the surface. If—no, *when* she found out who was sending them she intended telling them exactly what she thought of them!

When.

'I really would rather just forget all about it,' Jaz told Madelaine lightly.

'But is the person that's sending them going to do that?' came Madelaine's worried parting shot.

'Wake up, Jaz. I think it's time you and I had a little talk. In fact, from the look of this, it's past time!'

She recognized that grimly precise voice—how could she not, when it was the voice of the man she loved?—but as she fought her way through the layers of sleep back to consciousness she had no idea where she was. She barely knew who she was!

Although she did try to collect her scattered thoughts, slowly coming back to an awareness of her own comfortable armchair beneath her, of the glow of the fire through the delicate tissue of her lids.

'Jaz!' Beau encouraged determinedly, giving her arm a shake for good measure. 'I know you're awake, and

I'm not leaving here until you and I have talked, so you may as well stop pretending you're still asleep,' he added harshly.

How did he do that? She hadn't so much as moved, flickered an eyelash, and yet somehow he knew she was no longer asleep but fully aware of him in the sitting room of her little cottage. Quite how he had got there, she didn't yet know. But she intended finding out!

Besides, wasn't attack the best form of defence…?

Her lids snapped open as she glared up at him. 'What on earth do you think you're doing just walking in here?' she bit out irritably. 'I thought an Englishwoman's home was as much her castle as an Englishman's! Obviously I was wrong.' She gave him a pointed look as he seemed to fill half the tiny room with his sheer presence.

Beau gave a humourless smile. 'That's very good, Jaz,' he drawled. 'Angry indignation,' he mused. 'Pity it isn't working,' he added hardly.

No, she could see that it wasn't, Beau not in the least embarrassed or apologetic at having invaded her home in this way. In fact, he looked just as arrogantly confident as always.

'The back door was unlocked,' he continued hardly.

'So you just let yourself in,' she accused, struggling to sit up in the less-than-well-upholstered chair. A little dignity certainly wouldn't come amiss!

'I did knock first.' He shrugged. 'When you didn't answer, I tried the door—'

'And here you are!' she derided.

'Yes, here I am,' he confirmed slightly challengingly. 'Jaz, what, exactly, is this?'

Jaz felt the colour drain from her face as she looked at the crumpled piece of paper he held up in his hand.

Or, at least, it had been crumpled as she had hurled it angrily across the room an hour or so ago when she'd arrived back from Madelaine's; at this moment it was no longer crumpled but straightened out, and—worse—readable.

'Well?' he prompted at her continued silence.

She shrugged. 'It's an old scrap of paper,' she dismissed. 'I never was the best of housekeepers,' she added self-derisively, standing up and reaching out to take the sheet of paper, only to have Beau pull it out of her grasp. 'I was only going to throw it in the fire,' she reasoned lightly.

Beau looked at her searchingly, easily holding her gaze with his compelling one. 'What does it mean, Jaz?' he said softly.

'Mean?' she repeated mockingly. 'Why, I don't think it means anything. In fact, I don't even remember what it says—'

'Jaz,' he grated between gritted teeth. 'At the moment, I'm trying very hard to remain calm and reasonable—being treated like an idiot by you is not conducive to my remaining that way!'

Jaz's cheeks warmed at the deserved rebuke. Although how he knew that she was prevaricating, she had no idea—unless... 'Have you spoken to Madelaine?' she prompted suspiciously.

He raised dark brows. 'Since lunch-time? No,' he answered as she nodded. 'Should I have done?' he added sharply.

Jaz winced as she realized she was tying herself up in even more knots. 'No, of course not. I just—'

'Jaz, I'm not leaving here until I know what's going on,' he cut in forcefully. 'Why should Madelaine have spoken to me?'

'She shouldn't,' she snapped. 'I specifically asked her not to—' She broke off as she saw Beau's expression darken, not liking the way he thrust his empty hand into the back pocket of the black jeans he wore, either—as if he might strangle her if he didn't! 'Look, in the last couple of weeks I've had one or two silly letters delivered through my door—'

'How many?' he rasped, his expression grim. 'Is it one? Or is it two? Or is it more than that? Sorry?' he prompted hardly as she muttered a reply.

'I said it's four, including that one,' she raised her voice defensively. 'It's probably just a child playing silly games—'

'What did the other letters say?' Beau completely ignored her effort to dismiss the letters as unimportant, his eyes glittering dangerously silver.

Jaz gave a shrug of her narrow shoulders. 'Nothing of any—what do poison-pen—or, in this case, poison-computer!—letters usually say?' she said scathingly. 'Nothing that makes any sense to anyone but to the sender!'

'I wouldn't know, I've never received any,' he said softly.

'Well, I can assure you that's what they are—rubbish,' Jaz snapped impatiently, not at all enjoying this conversation, feeling completely on the defensive. Besides, it was none of Beau's business! 'Senseless,' she bit out scathingly. 'Completely senseless.'

Beau frowned. 'That night, the envelope you picked up from the doormat, the one you said was probably someone paying a bill, was that another of them?'

Not much escaped this man's notice. Or was forgotten...

She sighed. 'Yes.'

What else could she say? Besides, Beau had already warned her once about insulting his intelligence!

'And you knew it was too, didn't you?' he rasped.

She swallowed hard. 'Yes.'

His expression was grim as he looked down at the sheet of paper he still held in his hand. 'Why does this person accuse you of being a "liar"?'

'I don't know.' She shook her head.

She had wondered the same thing herself earlier, before she'd hurled the letter across the room. That accusation seemed to imply that she had done something she had said she wouldn't, that she had actually spoken to the person who was being so vindictive. And just the thought of that made her feel physically sick!

'I told you, Beau, it's all nonsense.' She moved restlessly.

'I won't know that until you tell me what the other letters said, now will I?' he reasoned in a deceptively mild tone, the nerve pulsing in his jaw indicative of his real mood. 'Or show me,' he added softly.

Jaz shakily released her breath. 'I don't have them. I either destroyed them or threw them away. I know, I know,' she muttered impatiently. 'Not a very sensible thing to do. Madelaine has already told me that once today!'

Beau straightened. 'You mentioned Madelaine before; does she know about these?' His hand tightened about the letter he still held.

'Yes, I spoke to her about them earlier,' Jaz snapped, standing up impatiently. Not that the room was really big enough for them both to stand up in, but she was tired of having Beau look down at her all the time.

Only to have Beau turn the tables on her by sitting down in the recently vacated chair and looking up at her instead, making Jaz feel like a naughty child before the headmaster, or an employee standing before the boss!

'Well, at least you seem to have done something sensible today,' he bit out scathingly.

'Thank you!' she scorned, eyes flashing deeply blue.

Beau sighed, shaking his head as he looked up at her. 'Why didn't you tell someone about them days ago? Why leave it all this time? Did you hope they were just going to go away? That the letters would just stop as suddenly as they began to arrive?'

'Yes, that's exactly what I hoped!' Jaz confirmed forcefully, moving back to stand before the fire.

He gave an impatient sigh. 'That isn't usually the way it works with these types of things. You—'

'I thought you said you had no experience of them?' Jaz cut in accusingly.

'I haven't. Not personally,' he conceded hardly. 'But I once did a documentary special and interviewed several people who do, from the sending as well as receiving end. And all the evidence pointed towards the fact that the people who send these types of letters get their enjoyment from watching the recipient squirm.'

She felt herself pale. 'Then they aren't being disappointed, are they?'

Beau gave her a considering look. 'That really depends how you look at it,' he said slowly. 'Obviously you've received the letters, because they were actually posted through your door, but, speaking as an outsider, I would say there has been very little public reaction from you to those letters. I certainly didn't know anything about them,' he added hardly.

Jaz's cheeks flushed. 'What was I supposed to do—

run out into the street thumping my chest and wailing at the unfairness of it all?'

His mouth twisted ruefully. 'Not as far as I'm concerned, no,' he assured her dryly. 'But to the person responsible for the letters? It would probably be a more satisfying reaction than the nothing you have given them so far.' He nodded.

She gave a pained frown. 'Do you really think so?'

'Don't you?'

She hadn't really thought about it, had been so intent on hiding the existence of those letters, and her response to them, that she hadn't really given the sender's reaction too much consideration.

But now that she did, she realized that Beau's comment was probably a fair one. Maybe that was the reason the letters had suddenly increased to two in one day? Maybe if she reacted—

What was she thinking? The person who had sent those letters to her was vicious and nasty, if not mentally unbalanced, and she had no intention of giving them the satisfaction of showing any response whatsoever!

'Maybe,' she conceded tightly. 'But I have no intention of doing so,' she assured him determinedly.

'Good for you.' Beau gave a tight smile. 'But in the meantime, do you think those letters are going to stop?'

She shrugged. 'Probably not.' Not until she either stopped seeing Beau or he left the village, that is!

'Do you have any idea what triggered them off in the first place?'

Jaz gave him a sharp look; was this man truly able to read her mind, or was she just so awful at hiding her thoughts?

'Jaz, when did the first letter arrive?' he prompted harshly.

She shook her head. 'I don't see—'

'When, Jaz?' he pushed determinedly.

Her mouth tightened. 'The day I began working for you—that was when the first one arrived, if you must know!'

His gaze narrowed. 'Oh, I think that I must,' he muttered icily. 'I remember how you looked that evening,' he rasped. 'I remember your making a joke about it, telling me you were pale because you had just received the electricity bill.'

She grimaced. 'I *had* just received the electricity bill, but the first of those letters was also amongst my post that day,' she continued before he could pounce again. 'And no—before you ask!—there was no stamp, and no date stamp, either; the letter had been hand-delivered to be opened with my other post of the day,' she added scornfully.

'Which means that the person delivering the letter must have known you wouldn't be there,' Beau murmured slowly.

'It seems a fair assumption to make, yes,' Jaz confirmed flatly.

She had been through all of this in her own mind so many times over the last week or so, had drawn exactly the same conclusion Beau was now doing—but still with no answer as to why anyone would be this vindictive to her.

'The day you began working for me, hmm?' he mused frowningly. 'What did that letter say?' he prompted shrewdly.

Jaz sat down with a sigh, knowing this man wasn't going anywhere until he had answers to all the questions he wanted to ask, and that she might as well at least be comfortable while she answered them. '"Like mother, like daughter",' she supplied flatly.

Beau's eyes narrowed to silver slits as he looked at her. 'Implying what?' he finally bit out abruptly.

She shrugged, her smile completely humourless. 'Implying that I'm like my mother, of course.'

'In what way?' he persued tersely.

'What way do you think?' she snapped, her eyes flashing deeply blue.

'I have no idea.' Beau shook his head. 'Okay, so your mother left your father and you when you were seventeen; she's far from the first woman to do so. And it wasn't as if you were still a baby or anything like that—'

'She left with someone else's husband!' Jaz cut in impatiently.

'Ah.' He nodded. 'You've never told me that before.'

'Why should I have done?' Jaz snapped accusingly.

'No particular reason.' He shrugged. 'But she's far from the first woman to do that, either,' he grimaced incomprehensively.

'In Aberton, she is,' Jaz assured him scathingly, the scandal having rocked the village for months, years, after her mother and her lover had died.

Beau gave her a rueful smile. 'Yes, I can believe that,' he continued briskly, 'the person sending these anonymous letters obviously believes that in some way you have become like your mother?'

'That would appear to be the case, yes.' She avoided his gaze, not wanting to see the scorn he must feel towards her mother, and possibly to her too...

'Because you're not only working for me, but we've

had a couple of meals together, too?' he murmured slowly.

'I think so, yes.'

Beau shook his head, frowning. 'But I'm not married.'

'I know.' She frowned her own confusion. 'But that doesn't seem to make a whole lot of difference.'

'No,' he agreed slowly. 'But who could it possibly matter to even if I were?'

'I don't know!' Jaz almost shouted with frustration.

'I'm sorry I have to ask these things, Jaz,' Beau told her ruefully. 'But if we're ever to discover who this person is, then we have to try and find out from what angle they are coming from.'

There seemed to be an awful lot of 'we's' in that statement…

'Has this ever happened before?' Beau grimaced. 'When you've been involved with anyone else,' he enlightened dryly as she looked puzzled.

Jaz glared at him. 'I've never been "involved" with anyone else—and, as you are only too well aware, I'm not involved with you, either,' she reminded him impatiently.

'This person obviously disagrees with you. Hmm, it's interesting.' He nodded distractedly.

Jaz's eyes widened indignantly. 'I don't find it in the least "interesting",' she told him furiously. 'Painful. Infuriating. Even disturbing. But never interesting!'

Beau gave her a sympathetic smile. 'That's because you aren't looking at this in the same way I am.'

As she had no idea how he was 'looking' at it, the answer to that was probably no!

She drew in a deep breath. 'Beau, could we just forget all about that for the moment while you tell me exactly why you came here to see me this evening?' She certainly hadn't got the impression from him earlier that they would be seeing each other again today. Or was it just a question of those magnets again, attracting him against his will...?

He stood up abruptly, his face set in grim lines as he walked over to stare down into the fire, his scar shown in stark relief.

'Beau...?' she prompted uncertainly as he didn't answer her but continued to look into the fire.

He drew in a sharp breath, straightened suddenly to turn and look at her, his hands thrust into the pockets of his denims. 'I came here this evening to tell you that I intend leaving Aberton on Saturday,' he bit out tautly.

Jaz's eyes widened in shock, and she could literally feel the colour leaving her cheeks as she continued to look at him, hoping he wasn't waiting for her to make some sort of comment on his statement—because at the moment her tongue felt as if it were stuck to the roof of her mouth, making speech impossible!

This was her worst nightmare come true—and so much quicker than even she could have imagined.

'Jaz?'

She swallowed hard. 'What about the house?'

'What about it?' he grimaced. 'Could you stand to live in it?'

'Me?' she gasped. 'No! But—'

'Neither can I,' he rasped. 'I'll sell it, eventually.' He shrugged. 'The house really isn't that important at the moment.'

Then what was? She didn't—

'Jaz, when I leave on Saturday I want you to come with me,' he bit out abruptly.

Jaz stared at him, totally beyond speech now. Totally beyond anything!

CHAPTER SIXTEEN

'WHY?' she prompted huskily.

Jaz had continued to stare at Beau for long, searching minutes, desperately trying to make sense of a conversation that had gone from discussing the anonymous poisonous letters she had been receiving, to Beau saying he wanted her to go with him when he left the village on Saturday.

The one thing that stood out crystal clear was that Beau hadn't told her why he wanted her to go with him. Was it just to help her get away from the village? Or was it something else...?

Beau frowned his impatience. 'Isn't it obvious?'

Jaz shook her head, her hair swinging silkily about her shoulders. 'Not to me, no.'

He shot her an irritated glance. 'Is this the usual way you respond to someone asking you to marry them?' he snapped.

Now she really was stunned. Beau was asking her to *marry* him?

Yes, that was exactly what he was doing, she acknowledged dazedly as she saw the look of grim determination on his face. But it was exactly that look that ensured she didn't jump up and throw her arms about him as she cried ecstatically: Yes, yes, yes! Because it wasn't the look of a man in love asking the woman he loved to be his wife and spend the rest of her life with him.

'I don't know,' she breathed softly. 'No one has ever asked me to marry them before. Why are *you* asking?'

He made an impatient movement. 'Jaz, think about it. You aren't coping here—'

'What?' she snapped as she stood up abruptly, her eyes glittering angrily as all her defences took over. 'How dare you come here and feel sorry for me?' she accused furiously. 'How dare you insult me by telling me you want me to marry you? In such a—an uninterested way! Am I supposed to be *grateful* for a proposal like that?'

He stiffened, his face set in cold mockery as he reached up and touched the livid scar on his cheek. 'I wasn't aware that I was insulting you,' he rasped scathingly. 'You're obviously drowning here, I'm leaving, I thought you might welcome the chance to get away yourself, and marrying me would be a way for you to do that. But if I was wrong—'

'You most definitely were!' Jaz bit out icily. 'I told you before, Beau, I'm not some charity case in need—' her voice broke with emotion '—in need,' she continued determinedly, 'of your pity!' She drew in a ragged breath, more hurt than she had ever believed possible. To be offered paradise in one hand, and know that it was only pity in the other!

He gave a derisive shake of his head. 'That isn't the way it looks from where I'm standing!'

'Then please leave,' she choked huskily. 'Just go,' she pleaded as he would have spoken again.

He moved stiffly to the door, pausing there. 'I'm leaving on Saturday afternoon,' he bit out abruptly. 'If you should change your mind—'

'I won't,' she assured him flatly, forcing herself to hold her head up high so that she met his gaze full on.

'I'll see that the outstanding money in your account is returned to you before you leave on Saturday.' Even if it would put her back in debt with the bank. She would rather starve herself for a month than be indebted to this man!

'Don't bother,' he scorned. 'I'm not going to miss it!'

'Neither am I,' she assured him defiantly.

He raised skeptical dark brows. 'As you wish,' he bit out tersely. 'I really don't care any more,' he told her icily before letting himself out of the cottage.

It was the fact that he didn't 'care' anything for her at all, besides pity, that had made her turn down his offer of marriage!

It was the fact that she 'cared' too much that she dropped down weakly into the armchair as soon as he had left, the tears falling hotly down her cheeks.

'Jaz, how lovely to see you!' Madelaine greeted warmly as the housekeeper ushered her guest into the sitting room. 'As you can see, dear Beau has decided to join us for tea too.' She gestured towards the man already occupying one of the armchairs.

Jaz had come to a halt in the doorway as soon as she'd spotted him in the room, eyeing him suspiciously as she'd hesitated about what to do next; it simply hadn't occurred to her that she and Madelaine wouldn't be having tea alone together. Beau's presence certainly complicated things.

'Jaz,' he greeted guardedly as he stood up, looking very handsome in black trousers, and a blue cashmere sweater over a paler blue shirt, his bland expression making it difficult to tell whether he was as surprised by her presence here as she was by his.

'Beau,' she returned stiffly.

'Do sit down, Jaz, darling,' Madelaine encouraged warmly, patting the seat next to her on the sofa.

Jaz hesitated, not happy with this situation at all. She hadn't seen Beau since that evening when he had told her he thought she should marry him—an offer she still felt no qualms about refusing!

But if he had kept to his original plan, then he was leaving tomorrow, and after that she would never see him again...

'Yes, do sit down, Jaz,' he encouraged dryly. 'If only so that I can do so too!'

She shot him a resentful glare, her cheeks feeling warm as she moved to sit on the edge of the sofa next to Madelaine.

Madelaine chuckled teasingly. 'You two have had a falling-out, haven't you?' She gave a reproving shake of her head. 'Everyone in the village is talking about it,' she added lightly.

Beau scowled. 'Then "everyone in the village" should learn to mind their own business!'

Madelaine smiled. 'But other people's business is always so much more interesting.'

'Do you think so?' Beau raised dark brows. 'Personally, I think they're a pretty uninspiring lot.'

'Is that why you're leaving?' Jaz shot at him challengingly.

'Leaving...?' Madelaine echoed huskily, staring at Beau, her face having gone slightly pale. 'But—I had no idea.' She looked at him accusingly.

'No, it isn't public knowledge yet,' he drawled, giving Jaz a look that clearly said *Thanks!*

'But Jaz knows,' Madelaine pointed out.

'Well…yes,' Beau confirmed lightly. 'But, then, she would, wouldn't she?'

'Why would she?' Madelaine frowned.

He shrugged. 'Because she's going with me.'

Jaz looked at him sharply. He knew she wasn't going anywhere with him, tomorrow or any other time. What was he doing? More to the point, did he have any idea what he was doing?

'What?' Madelaine gasped, standing up to look down at Jaz accusingly. 'That is so sly,' she said harshly. 'And you never said a word. Not a single word! How could you, Jaz? How could you?'

'How could she what, Madelaine?' Beau was the one to answer her mildly.

Jaz made a silencing gesture in his direction; he was just making this so much more difficult than it already was. 'Beau, please—'

'Madelaine?' he prompted hardly, his attention all focused on the other woman.

The beautiful face was twisted with anger, the eyes glittering furiously, the slender hands clenched into fists. 'You are so like your mother, Jaz,' Madelaine bit out scathingly. 'Not only do you look like her—'

'I do not!' Jaz cut in compulsively.

'Oh yes, you do.' The older woman's dislike was written clearly in her face as she looked down at Jaz. 'She had that wild beauty too. Untamed. Gypsyish.' Her top lip curled back disdainfully. 'Charles told me that comparing the two of us was like being with fire and ice.' And there was no doubt which one Madelaine thought the more attractive.

Jaz stared at the other woman, her emotions a mixture of distaste, sadness and pity.

Distaste, because after talking with Beau the other

night, about what possible motive someone could have for writing those horrible letters to her, Jaz had painfully worked out by a process of elimination that there was only one person who really fitted that description; Madelaine, the woman whose husband, Charles, had left her to be with Janie, Jaz's mother.

Sadness, because all these years she had really thought Madelaine had been her friend.

And pity, because Madelaine must have harboured this resentment and pain all these years, to the point that her emotions had been warped by it.

Jaz's eyes widened as she looked at Beau, seeing her own emotions reflected on his face as he looked at the other woman, realizing at that moment that his conversation just now hadn't been innocently provocative at all, that somehow Beau had worked out exactly who it was who was sending her those horrible letters—and decided to confront Madelaine with it before he left!

The fact that Jaz had come here today with the same intention was incredible.

Beau stood up now, carefully placing himself between Jaz and Madelaine, it seemed. 'Why did you do it, Madelaine?' he prompted gruffly. 'What possible harm has Jaz ever done to you?'

'Harm?' the older woman echoed scathingly. 'Her mother stole my husband, took him away from me!' Her pointed chin rose challengingly. 'Charles would have eventually returned to me once he realized what sort of woman Janie Logan was,' she said with conviction. 'But instead he was killed in a car accident. With her mother!' Blue eyes glittered with hatred as she looked at Jaz.

Jaz flinched back in the chair at the vitriol now pouring out of the woman she had always thought was her friend, never having dreamt that this was the way Madelaine really felt about what had happened eight years ago.

It had been such an awful time for those left behind, for Jaz and her father, for Madelaine, and somehow quite natural for Madelaine and Jaz to gravitate towards each other in their loss, for the two of them to become friends. And all this time, it seemed, Madelaine had been harbouring these feelings of resentment and hatred.

Feelings that couldn't be vented on Janie or Charles because they were both dead, but could certainly be felt by Janie's daughter…!

Jaz felt slightly sick at having her suspicions proved correct, had been hoping—inwardly pleading!—for her assessment of the situation to be the wrong one.

But she had gone through every person in the village who she thought could possibly have a motive for sending her those letters, especially that last one, the one that even Beau had realized implied she had deliberately lied about something.

And the only thing Jaz could think of that someone could possibly accuse her of lying about was her feelings towards Beau, and even those hadn't exactly been lies, just self-defence. But the only person she had expressed those feelings to was Madelaine—Madelaine who had kept questioning her on the subject, kept suggesting that she should be wary of Beau…

'But Jaz wasn't responsible for any of that, Madelaine,' Beau spoke to her soothingly. 'She was just a child, hurt herself by what had happened.'

Madelaine glared at him. 'She deserved to be hurt, her and her father! If John Logan had kept his wife under control none of this would have happened, and I would still have my husband. But instead I've been left smouldering here for the last eight years, apparently wealthy, but all the time the money that Charles left me has been rapidly depleting—'

'But another rich husband would have changed all that…?' Beau prompted softly.

'Yes,' Madelaine confirmed scornfully. 'But instead I've had to sit here and watch her, Janie Logan's daughter—' she gave Jaz a vicious look '—captivate the only decent man to come to the area in years!'

Beau…

Jaz's feeling of nausea intensified. It was bad enough to know that this was the way Madelaine had really felt all these years, but to realize it was her own apparent friendship with Beau that had triggered the other woman's hatred onto a new level was so awful Jaz just didn't know what to say or do.

Beau, fortunately, felt no such inhibitions. 'Even without Jaz I wouldn't have been interested, Madelaine,' he rasped. 'You simply aren't my type.'

Madelaine gave a dismissive shake of her head. 'You're only saying that because *she's* here—'

'No, Madelaine,' he cut in calmly. 'I'm saying it because it's the truth—I don't think so!' he snapped as Madelaine moved to rake her long red fingernails down his face, grasping both her arms and easily holding her away from him, his expression now grim with distaste.

'Maybe you deserve each other, after all!' Madelaine spat the words at him, her pretty face ugly in her vehemence as she struggled to free herself—and didn't succeed.

Beau shrugged unconcernedly. 'Maybe we do, but that really isn't for you to say, now is it?' he reasoned gently.

Madelaine looked at him through narrowed lids. 'You think you're so clever, don't you?' she scorned. 'Both of you!' She gave Jaz a look of intense dislike.

'Jaz has nothing to do with any of this,' Beau answered her evenly. 'She was as much an innocent bystander as you were. Can't you see that?'

Several emotions followed in quick succession across Madelaine's distorted face; anger, frustration, pain. It was the latter that finally won out as her face crumpled and the tears began to fall.

Jaz moved as if to stand up, but Beau motioned for her to remain where she was, still holding Madelaine in his grip.

'You need to talk to someone, Madelaine,' he told her huskily. 'Someone with professional expertise. If I call a friend of mine, a psychiatrist, will you agree to see him?'

Jaz looked at him with admiring eyes; she had been wondering where all this was going to end, knew that they couldn't just leave here today without resolving this situation in some way, that Madelaine needed help of some sort—but at the same time knowing she didn't have the means or contacts to provide that help.

Madelaine looked up dazedly, her make-up blotchy on her face, looking every one of her forty-five years at that moment. 'Do you mean to call the police, too?' she said gruffly.

'No, I don't think that's necessary.' Beau gave a tight smile. 'I don't think either Jaz or I want it to come to that…?' He gave Jaz a questioning look.

'No,' she hastened to assure them both, sitting forward in her armchair once again. 'No,' she repeated gently, her gaze compassionate as it rested on Madelaine.

Who would have ever guessed, from the beautiful and confidant façade Madelaine liked to present to the world, that she had so much hate and bitterness inside her? Jaz certainly hadn't!

Jaz stood up. 'I'm really sorry, Madelaine,' she murmured huskily. 'For what my mother did to you. For what you thought I was doing to you.' She gave a confused shake of her head. 'I really don't know what else to say.'

And she didn't, knew that now this was all over, completely out in the open, she just wanted to get away from here, to lick her own wounds.

Beau released Madelaine, the other woman dropping down into one of the armchairs, looking suddenly frail and older than her years. 'Yes, it's time we were going, Madelaine,' he told her evenly as he reached out and gently pulled Jaz to his side. 'I'll have my friend telephone you later, shall I?' he prompted softly.

Madelaine looked up dazedly. 'Yes. Yes… I—I'm sorry, Jaz. It really wasn't… I just—' She gave a confused shake of her head, as if just waking from a dream—or a nightmare.

'We really do have to go, Madelaine,' Beau cut in briskly, obviously having felt Jaz tremble at his side and guessed how close she was to falling apart herself.

It had all been just too much for Jaz, her suspicions, having those suspicions confirmed with such bitter anger, and the reason behind them. She had never guessed, never even considered—

'Come on, Jaz,' Beau prompted firmly, his arm about her waist as he guided her from the room and the house before she collapsed completely under the strain.

CHAPTER SEVENTEEN

'How did you know it was Madelaine?' Jaz prompted huskily.

Beau had driven the two of them to Jaz's cottage, silently making them both a cup of strong tea before seating them both comfortably in the sitting room.

He sat in the armchair across from her now, his expression still grim. 'Purely by accident, as it happens,' he rasped, shaking his head disgustedly. 'Barbara Scott, at the shop, happened to mention to me this morning how wonderful it was that you and Madelaine had become such friends after the upset eight years ago.' He gave Jaz a censorious look. 'Didn't you think it was important, in the circumstances, to tell me that it was Madelaine's husband your mother ran away with when she left the village?'

Jaz could feel the warmth in her cheeks. 'It never even occurred to me that you needed to know,' she told him honestly. 'I never thought—I had no idea—' She broke off, shaking her head dazedly.

'But you knew Madelaine was the one sending those letters before you went to have tea with her today, didn't you?' he rasped.

'Yes,' she confirmed huskily.

'But you went anyway,' he snapped angrily. 'Jaz, do you have any idea of the danger you put yourself in? It must be obvious to you by now that Madelaine had been seriously unbalanced by this whole thing? That the situation could have turned very nasty—'

'I was hoping I was wrong!' she cried emotionally.

Beau drew in a deeply controlling breath, letting it out again with a heavy sigh. 'You scare the hell out of me, do you know that?' he muttered impatiently.

Her eyes widened. 'I do?'

'You do,' he confirmed harshly, standing up in forceful movements. 'How am I supposed to leave here tomorrow when all the time I'm going to be worried what might happen to you next?' He looked at her accusingly.

Jaz frowned her confusion. 'But Madelaine has agreed to get help. Do you think she might renege on that agreement?' she added worriedly.

He gave a confident shake of his head. 'I'll make sure she doesn't get the chance!' he assured her grimly.

'Then why should you worry about me…?' Jaz said slowly, still totally confused.

'Because I seem to have done little else since I moved here!' he bit out disgustedly. 'Your obviously unhappy childhood with what I would guess were overstrict grandparents. The fact that your mother walked out on you when you were seventeen. Your father dying. This situation with Madelaine. A damned tile falling off a roof!' he added exasperatedly.

Jaz eyed him dazedly. He wasn't wrong about her childhood, or any of the other things, but what on earth did a tile falling off a roof have to do with anything? Let alone to the point that Beau worried about it…!

'Beau…?' she prompted hesitantly.

'Jaz!' he came back irritably, glaring his frustration at her, his hands tightly clenched at his sides.

Jaz felt the ice start to melt about her heart, to feel a new hope, an anticipation that perhaps everything was going to work out okay after all. 'Beau, why did you ask me to marry you?' she prompted huskily, hoping she wasn't wrong, hoping that she didn't have to resurrect that barrier about her heart.

'Surely that's obvious?' he came back defensively.

'You said that the last time I asked.' She shook her head. 'It isn't a good enough answer.'

'Oh isn't it?' He gave a humourless smile. 'What is it you want to hear, Jaz? Hearts and roses? Would you believe me if I were to say any of those flowery things?'

She swallowed hard. 'If you say them, I'll believe them.'

His eyes narrowed. 'Even if they're not true?'

He was so defensive. Too defensive.

'But they are true, aren't they, Beau?' Jaz took the biggest risk of her young life, knowing if he pushed her away now that she couldn't bear it. 'I love you, Beauregard Garrett,' she told him huskily, her gaze unwavering on his.

'You—' he gasped disbelievingly, shaking his head in confusion. 'But the other day you said—you told me—' He broke off abruptly. 'No, you didn't say anything at all, did you, except that you wouldn't marry me if all I felt for you was pity?' he realized self-disgustedly. 'Jaz, I don't pity you,' he groaned. 'I love you. I love you so much I can't think of anything else!'

The ice melted totally within her, leaving only a warm rush of love. 'Why couldn't you have told me that the other evening?' she said achingly, her eyes brimming with tears—but tears of happiness this time. 'Why, Beau?'

A nerve pulsed in his jaw, throwing his scar into livid profile. 'Because of this.' His hand moved instinctively to that scar. 'Once you had told me that you found my marriage proposal an insult, I—' He shook his head, staring down at her intently. 'Jaz, did you just tell me that you love me?'

'Oh, yes,' she breathed ecstatically as she stood up to move into his waiting arms. 'I love you so much,' she assured him. 'I just want to be with you for ever.'

He hesitated. 'I'm much older than you. And the scar—'

'I'm not interested in that silly old scar,' she dismissed uncaringly. 'I feel sorry for the television executives because they are!' she added.

'But they aren't,' Beau told her ruefully. 'I was the one who refused to renew my contract.'

Jaz's eyes widened. 'You were?'

'Yes,' he confirmed tersely. 'But we can discuss that later. A long time later,' he added huskily as his head bent towards hers. 'Right now I want to kiss my fiancée.' He smiled, looking almost boyish. 'That sounds good, doesn't it?' he said with satisfaction.

'Very good,' Jaz concurred, her body curving into his.

'Except…' Beau became very still, his mouth only inches away from hers.

'Except?' Jaz eyed him warily, still not a hundred per cent certain that this happiness could really be hers.

'I still haven't asked you properly,' he muttered self-derisively. 'Jaz, I love you to distraction, want to spend the rest of my life with you, to have you to look after, and for you to look after me; will you marry me?'

'Oh, yes,' she breathed without hesitation.

It was a long time later that they talked again, a very long time later, the two of them laying on the sofa, Jaz's face flushed from their lovemaking as she lay in Beau's arms.

'Tell me about your mother,' he encouraged gruffly.

She didn't stiffen as she usually did when her mother was mentioned, instead smiling sadly. 'She was seventeen when my father, a man fifteen years older than her, moved into the village and opened up the garden centre.' She grimaced. 'According to my grandparents she was always wild, wanting to escape the cloying atmosphere of the vicarage, I suppose, and John Logan represented that escape. Within three months of his moving here, my mother was pregnant. A month later they were married. Three months or so after that, before I was even born, my mother realized she had made a mistake, that she had just escaped one prison for another.' Jaz shrugged. 'But it was too late, of course.'

Beau shook his head slowly. 'You must have heard most of that second, even third hand?'

'I suppose,' she conceded ruefully. 'But my mother was certainly unhappy, that I do know.'

'Maybe, and yet she didn't leave until you were seventeen,' he pointed out gently.

'No,' Jaz accepted slowly.

'When she left, with Charles Wilder...' Beau frowned, absently playing with the hair at Jaz's temple '...did she say anything to you, or did she just up and go?'

'She just—no,' Jaz corrected breathlessly. 'She left me a letter, told me that she was sorry, that once she was settled with—with Charles, that she would send for me.'

'And?' Beau prompted gently.

Jaz let out a shaky breath. 'They were killed three months later before they could settle anywhere. Beau, do you think—?'

'I think your mother loved you, Jaz.' He moved so

that he was looking down at her, his gaze intent on the flushed beauty of her face. 'Your grandparents, as you've already told me, were hopelessly inadequate to bring up a daughter—let alone a granddaughter! Your father—well, I'm not sure I can speak for your father, but if Janie was anything like you to look at—'

'She was.' Jaz nodded, knowing that she had been angry with Madelaine earlier because she knew she looked like her mother.

Beau reached out and touched the softness of her lips. 'Then he must have gone through the torments of hell knowing she had only married him to escape her overbearing parents,' he grated.

She reached up and entwined her arms about the back of his head, holding him securely in her arms. 'Whereas I am marrying you because I love you so much I just want to spend the rest of my life with you,' she told him with husky honesty.

'Oh, Jaz!' His arms tightened about her. 'Can you bear to leave here and live in London with me?' He looked down at her anxiously. 'I went back last weekend to discuss a new contract, one where I can get back to the investigative reporting that I used to love,' he explained at her questioning look. 'Lying in the hospital after the accident, the weeks afterwards, I realized that I had to make changes in my life, that there was no longer any challenge to what I was doing. Although loving you as part of that challenge wasn't something I initially welcomed!' he acknowledged with a self-mocking grin.

Jaz did her best to hold back a smile—and failed miserably. 'Poor Beau,' she grinned unabashedly.

'Lucky Beau,' he corrected. 'Happy Beau. Ecstatic Beau!' he assured her with a grin. 'The network has offered me a six-month contract, twelve programmes, investigating whatever I feel like investigating. But it means moving back to London, and if that isn't agreeable to you then I'll simply tell them I can't do it—'

'Of course it's agreeable to me,' Jaz assured him happily, but pleased that he took her needs so much into consideration. 'I don't care where I am as long as I'm with you. Besides,' she added teasingly, 'I've already agreed to sell this cottage and the land to a neighbouring farmer. He takes over at the end of the month.'

'He—' Beau broke off incredulously. 'Where were you going, Jaz? What were you going to do?' He frowned.

She shrugged. 'Well, the farmer agreed to give me quite a bit more money than I expected, so I had thought about travelling for a while, maybe eventually settling somewhere in France or Spain. After all, they need gardeners over there too, and—'

'You were just going to leave here without telling me where you were going?' Beau groaned incredulously.

'I didn't know where I was going—or that you would be interested,' she pointed out softly.

'You, madam, are going nowhere—unless I can come too,' he told her determinedly. 'If you really want to travel, then we can. It might be fun at that,' he added reflectively.

'And your new contract?'

'It can wait. The only thing that matters to me is you, Jaz, you and your happiness,' he told her intently.

And the only thing that mattered to her was Beau's happiness. Besides, the travel idea had just been something for her to do in order to try and get over loving Beau. How wonderful that she didn't have to get over it, after all!

'Then we'll go to London,' she told him happily. 'I've never been there, either,' she confided. 'And maybe some time soon we might think about children…?' It was her dearest wish, having been an only child, to have a houseful of her own, but she had no idea how Beau felt about children at all…

'Mary or Mark?' he remembered teasingly.

Jaz smiled. 'Well…I may just change my mind about that.'

'As long as you don't change your mind about loving me!' he said intently.

'Never,' she assured him confidently.

Beau was everything she wanted, or would ever want, and as she looked into his eyes, at the love glowing there for her, she knew that he felt the same way about her.

It was everything.

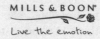

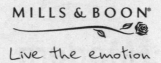

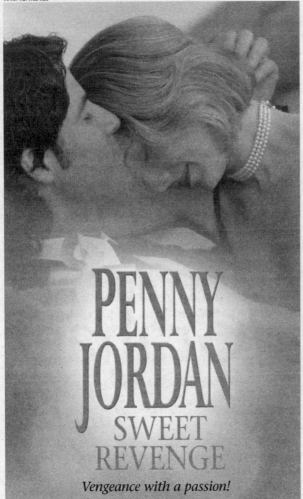

PENNY JORDAN

SWEET REVENGE

Vengeance with a passion!

On sale 4th March 2005

Available at most branches of WHSmith, Tesco, ASDA, Martins, Borders, Eason, Sainsbury's and all good paperback bookshops.

MILLS & BOON

**Volume 9
on sale from
5th March
2005**

Lynne
Graham

International Playboys

*Angel of
Darkness*

FREE

4 BOOKS AND A SURPRISE GIFT!

We would like to take this opportunity to thank you for reading this Mills & Boon® book by offering you the chance to take FOUR more specially selected titles from the Modern Romance™ series absolutely FREE! We're also making this offer to introduce you to the benefits of the Reader Service™—

- ★ **FREE home delivery**
- ★ **FREE gifts and competitions**
- ★ **FREE monthly Newsletter**
- ★ **Books available before they're in the shops**
- ★ **Exclusive Reader Service offers**

Accepting these FREE books and gift places you under no obligation to buy; you may cancel at any time, even after receiving your free shipment. Simply complete your details below and return the entire page to the address below. You don't even need a stamp!

YES! Please send me 4 free Modern Romance books and a surprise gift. I understand that unless you hear from me, I will receive 6 superb new titles every month for just £2.69 each, postage and packing free. I am under no obligation to purchase any books and may cancel my subscription at any time. The free books and gift will be mine to keep in any case.

P5ZEE

Ms/Mrs/Miss/Mr.............................Initials ....
BLOCK CAPITALS PLEASE

Surname ....

Address ....

....

....Postcode ....

Send this whole page to:

The Reader Service, FREEPOST CN81, Croydon, CR9 3WZ

WIN a romantic weekend in PARiS

To celebrate Valentine's Day we are offering you the chance to WIN one of 3 romantic weekend breaks to Paris.

✄

Imagine you're in Paris; strolling down the Champs Elysées, pottering through the Latin Quarter or taking an evening cruise down the Seine. Whatever your mood, Paris has something to offer everyone.

For your chance to make this dream a reality simply enter this prize draw by filling in the entry form below:

Name _____

Address _____

_____ Tel no: _____

Closing date for entries is 30th June 2005

Please send your entry to:

Valentine's Day Prize Draw
PO Box 676, Richmond, Surrey, TW9 1WU